Westward Wanderers

-BOOK TWO-

The Dawn Wakers

Angela Castillo

To Jacob. My dawn waker.

And to Evelyn, Gloria, Charisse and Sarah,
who have faithfully proofread
almost every book I have written.
Words cannot express my thankfulness.

Author's Note

Much debate is held over how churches operated in the early west. Many denominations had committees and organizations early on to appoint pastors to specific 'posts.' Also, circuit riders–ministers who rode to various towns on a schedule–served many areas where congregations could not secure a permanent pastor of their own.

I have imagined a scenario with a small town, an abandoned church, and what it would look like if a man of God rode in to 'volunteer' his ministry. To the best of my knowledge and research, the scenario I've presented is a plausible one.

PART ONE

I

A Monument of Names

Independence Rock loomed in the distant horizon, round and lumpy, like a giant turtle rising above the shining Sweetwater River. Ellie failed to understand the attraction, since she'd been subjected to boulders of every shape and size for the last three months. A stand of trees would hold more fascination, a rare enough site on the trail for several weeks now.

At least she was free for a short while. Free from small, sticky hands grasping at her skirts. The incessant babble of shrill voices, the endless need.

Thaddeus Herschel strode a few steps before her, eyes trained on the sparse path through the thick, scrubby grass, thin fingers clasped behind his back. Normally he'd share a joke or quiet conversation, but today he didn't speak.

Ellie empathized with his need for space. For much of this journey, she'd drifted off to lands of her own imagining. Places from fairy books, with tropical plants and cool waterfall grottos; not barren, sand-covered plains holding death and unyielding sameness.

Stan Wilkens led the small group of young people from the wagon train, with Francie, Thaddeus's sister, holding to his elbow like a thirsty tick on a dog. Stan bobbed his head to Francie's high, giggling contributions to the conversation. Occasionally he'd glance back at the rest of the group as though imploring for someone to rescue him.

Francie had been the one to invite Ellie in the first place, though Ellie was uncertain if her motives more from pity than friendship. Though both girls were eighteen, they had little else in common.

Lagging behind Ellie, at the end of the small party, were Maggie, Thaddeus's youngest sister, and her friend, Felicity Martin. They whispered behind their hands, discussing matters only important to girls of fourteen. *I should make sure they don't dawdle on the path.* She was weary, bone weary of watching. More than anything she desired a delicious moment of unfettered, deliberate abandon.

"Ellie, get ahold of yourself," she murmured. "Complaining never helped anything."

Thaddeus swiveled, allowing her to catch up. He gazed down at her. "What was that, Ellie?"

Ellie's heart gave a teensy flutter. Thaddeus's light blue eyes contrasted the dark hair that fell over his brow whenever he removed his hat. None of the men on the trail had seen a barber since Missouri, but the scruffy look suited Thaddeus. A worn suit coat hung on his shoulders, oversized like most of the clothes belonging to the folks of the wagon train. On the trail, only the most essential mending could be managed and tailoring for adjustments was out of the question.

"Oh, I didn't mean to say that out loud," Ellie replied. "My thoughts must be running ahead of me again."

Thaddeus's mouth quirked up under his beard. "After all this time on the trail, most of us deal with that malady on occasion." He raised an eyebrow. "Are you feeling well? It'll be another while before we reach the rock, and I've heard it's quite a climb."

"I'll be fine," Ellie reassured him. "I've become stronger in the last few months. Jerusha's medicine has helped me more than any of the doctors in Missouri." She wrinkled her nose. "I don't know what she puts in that stuff. The nastiest draught you could imagine, but it's a powerful help."

"I'm glad." The twinkle in Thaddeus's eyes supported his words.

Ellie would have believed him anyway. Thaddeus was kinder than any man she'd known. Even kinder than Shiloh, her friend Ami's husband.

Ami. She swallowed. Where was Ami? The girl who'd joined the wagon train to help care for Ellie's brothers and sisters had suddenly married a wagon scout and left the group to head for Montana. *Lord, keep her safe.* Ellie sent up the automatic prayer that always came with thoughts of her friend. Ellie had given Ami the address of the Oregon homestead where her father and two brothers waited for them. Hopefully a letter from Ami would beat them there.

Three months until we arrive, if not longer. Ellie shivered despite the heat. *How will we ever make it?*

The party reached the shadow of the great rock. When Ellie squinted, she could see them. Names like scars on its surface. Some were etched on with a sharp tool, while several appeared to be written with pitch. Many were carved in shaky, illegible figures, and some were presented in swooping letters, like fancy ladies dancing across the granite surface.

Many folks who couldn't write their own names, but still felt the need to leave permanent evidence they'd accomplished the journey had signed their names with a simple X. Captain Marshall had said people wrote them for luck. Ellie wondered how many of these hopeful souls had ended up scalped or floating in a pool of alkali.

Ellie had no use for luck. Her faith was placed in the Lord, as always from when she'd been a little girl.

Her mother was different. Sometimes she reached back to the recesses of her German ancestors, the ones who believed in fate and spirits and fortune. Martha Davis's Bible had four-leafed clovers pressed between the leaves. "I trust the Almighty. However, I'm not taking any chances," she'd say.

Over the last few days, her mother had settled into a sullen mood. Ellie had been shocked when she'd agreed to let her join the little expedition to the boulders. "Don't forget to put my name too," Mother had snapped. "Goodness knows I need all the luck I can get."

Ellie slipped on a loose stone and wobbled.

Thaddeus caught her elbow to steady her. "Are you sure you're all right?"

"Clumsy me." *Ellie, you'd better focus on the path before you turn an ankle and must be mercy shot right here in the dirt. Mother would never recover.*

Stan beckoned to the group, a bucket of axle grease dangling from his arm. "Let's move further down and find an open space."

Everyone scrambled after him in a tight line except for Francie, who hung back. Ellie suspected she feared grease splatters.

After scrambles over rocks and thrashing through brambles, Stan found a smooth, clear area on the rock. "This will do," he announced grandly.

Maggie tapped Ellie's shoulder. "What are you going to write?"

"My name, I suppose," said Ellie.

Maggie tossed her curls. "I thought you'd write something fancy, since you're always making up pretty stories and poems."

Ellie pointed to Stan, who'd managed to scrape out the four letters of his first name. "It seems a bit tricky for all that. And the grease is messy."

Maggie stared down at her hands, slender, white, and dotted with small, hardened spots. "I hadn't thought of that. I'm glad I chose not to wear gloves. They're the last pair I have left."

Ellie didn't answer. Her fingers, twisted into her apron, were leathered and brown as a man's. They'd been that way even before the start of the trail. A poor girl, especially the oldest of seven children, didn't have the luxury of keeping her hands nice.

Finally, the dripping brush came to Thaddeus. He painted his signature in strong, bold lettering, followed by a cross. When he passed the sticky brush to Ellie, she wrote her name, then added a shaky 'Martha' as she'd promised, though Mother would never see it.

Dutiful. That's who I am.

She let out a long, ranging sigh, then noticed everyone's eyes fixed on her face.

"Are you feeling quite right, dear?" Francie said in the sugary-sweet tone she always used when addressing her.

"I'm fine," Ellie replied.

The two younger girls added their names to the list.

Maggie held the brush out to her sister. "Come on, Francie. You came all this way. A little pitch never hurt anyone."

Francie wrote a mincing "F.H.," holding the brush as far as her arm could extend. "There!" she said, dropping the brush on the ground. "I've done it. No one can say I didn't."

"This brush belongs to my father." Stan glared at her, retrieved the tool, and dropped it into the grease bucket. "We'd better head back for chore time. Father threatened to tan my hide if I dawdled here for too long."

"Why, Stan Wilkins," Francie cooed, taking his arm once again. "You're twenty years old if you're a day. Would your father really give you a whipping?"

"I don't reckon I want to find out." Stan shook off her hand and stalked back to the trail.

The sun beat down mercilessly, and the group moved quickly, following scant patches of shade created by larger bushes and scrub.

Ellie counted heads; a habit created from being the oldest of an ever-growing brood. "Thaddeus, where are Maggie and Felicity?"

Thaddeus glanced behind her and rolled his eyes. "Wait up," he called to the rest of the group.

He disappeared through the brush once more. "Maggie, we need to get going, come on!"

Ellie's chest tightened. If she didn't get home, her mother would never let her out like this again. Not ever. She'd always refer to the 'time you didn't come back when I told you.' Should she set off on her own? The wagons were a good twenty-minute walk from here and safety was to be found in numbers . . . especially this close to dusk.

She darted a glance to the others. Francie hummed a little tune and picked burrs off her apron strings, while Stan stared at his feet, his face deepening in shades of red.

"We're coming. Felicity found an interesting rock and I wanted it for my collection. We had to pry it out, that's all." Maggie's protests echoed off the canyon walls.

"Next time tell us where you're going," Thaddeus replied in a patient, big brotherly tone.

He glanced at Stan and Ellie. "Sorry about that. Let's head on back."

Clouds blew over their heads, creating shadows that stretched out across the brush-covered land. The circle of schooners on the plain below them were like toys, with tiny doll people scurrying about. Far beyond their clump of wagons was a smaller circle several miles away, also camped for the night, all hugging the banks of the river.

And behind them another train, and behind them another. An endless line of people seeking their fortunes in a strange new land, many of them to find an early grave instead of a brave new bounty.

Don't be so morbid, Ellie.

The younger girls passed her now. A familiar catch plugged her chest, and her breaths came a bit shorter.

Thaddeus glanced behind and slowed, allowing the chatting girls to pass.

"May I walk with you?"

Ellie tipped her head to the side. "I'd like that."

Thaddeus caught up some flowers as they walked, mostly the scrubby desert varieties with barely a hint of color, along with a few hardy orange blooms. He arranged these into a small posy.

"How pretty," said Ellie. "Are those for your mother?"

Thaddeus squinted at them. "No, she only wants the hothouse flowers one can buy from a stand. I thought . . ." He held them out. "Would you like them?"

"Thank you." Ellie took them and breathed in the dusty, honey-like aroma. "It's nice to find such lovely things in the cracked rocks."

Thaddeus nodded. "And God knows each one. He knows each flower that blooms, even though the human eye may never see them, from seed to withered stalk."

"I've never considered that, but it must be true," said Ellie. "It's a lovely thought."

"Isn't it though?" Thaddeus took off his hat and wiped his brow with a handkerchief. "I'm glad you came with us today, Ellie. You work so hard."

Ellie ducked her head. "I am the poor, pitiful sick girl, aren't I?"

He crossed his arms. "I'm sorry. Forgive me for my forwardness."

"Oh, nothing to be sorry for, Thaddeus." Remorse stung her lips. "It follows me always. Sometimes I feel like I might as well be wearing a sandwich board, advertising to the world." As she spoke, she wondered why she'd be sharing this hapless information with any soul, even Thaddeus.

"I don't think of you like that, Ellie," he said quietly.

They had almost reached the makeshift pasture where oxen, cows and horses greedily ate the thick prairie grass that grew in abundance around the banks of the Sweetwater.

Ellie placed a light hand on Thaddeus's arm. "Thank you. You're right, you know. Sometimes I need to be free."

Mother sloshed the last bit of soup into Ellie's bowl and rocked back on her heels. "The boys were ornery as ever. I'm happy you managed to reach the rock after all." Her eyes crinkled at the corners and she wrapped Ellie in a thick hug, causing her spoon to clatter against the sides of the bowl. "You are managing, despite the hardships." A tear dripped down the end of her nose and she brushed it away. "Your father will be glad to see you with us. When we decided to follow him to Oregon, I knew it would be a struggle for you. Thought about leaving you with Aunt Lorianne, but I couldn't bear to come without all of my children."

Ellie squirmed on the rock that served for a chair. She wished Mother wouldn't discuss her health so flippantly. Since her bout with the fever a year ago, the sickness had always been a point of interest. Back home in Missouri, Mother would mention it during a lull in conversation with friends and family. The old women made tsking sounds behind their teeth, and the young ladies gave sympathetic nods, all the time watching her as though they expected her to drop dead at any moment.

As a middle-aged woman with seven children, Martha Davis basked in attention and sympathy. These situations made Ellie want to shrink down and hide away.

"Nice flowers." Mother pointed to the small, already wilting posy Ellie had thrust through the top buttonhole of her shirtwaist. "Never see you gathering them."

"Mm-hmm." Ellie decided not to explain the origin of the blossoms, since her mother would be quick to pounce on any indication someone was 'sweet on' her daughter. Ellie couldn't abide another lecture on how she was 'too weak to be a wife.' She'd heard it any time a man gave her the slightest glance of admiration.

The haze of dusk fell over the family. Dan and Dave, four and five, whittled impossible creatures from scraps of wood. Ivy, though a bit old for dolls at eight, cradled an ancient rag baby that had once belonged to Ellie.

"Tell a story, Ellie, please do," begged Ivy.

Ellie hesitated, her weariness from the day's walk weighing her down like a thick shawl.

Tiny Heston, Ellie's two-year-old brother, curled sticky fingers around her hand. Ellie set the empty soup bowl aside, wishing for more. She pulled the tot, damp with sweat and covered from head to toe in dust, into her lap. "Of course I'll tell a story, my darlings."

Heston rested his bright blond curls against her shoulder and popped his thumb into his mouth.

Mother busied herself clearing supper, while Ellie's siblings listened with bright eyes and clasped hands as Ellie began her story.

Though she borrowed heavily from the fairy stories she'd read in school, every tale was different.

"Once upon a time, there was a princess who wanted to be strong. She travelled to a wise old woman to ask for advice . . ."

Her words swelled into the night to join the multitude of tales, songs and prayers rising like smoke from the dozens of campfires around them. The chorus of voices pulsed through her soul, the constant reassurance that they possessed more than the drive to put one foot before the other. These vocal entreaties carried their spirits forth like ships in the darkness, with the bright light of hope to push them to their destination.

2
Cow Chips and Songs

Morning sunshine cut through the thin walls of the canvas tent. Ellie groaned and rolled over, pulling a worn quilt over her head. Ivy didn't stir beside her.

Though Ellie missed Ami, she had to admit the tent was roomier now. With barely enough space for two, the three of them had been packed in like canned oysters. On the nights Heston would crawl inside and cuddle with them, sleep had been near impossible.

She dressed quickly. Nights grew chillier the closer they came to the mountains, but by morning her clothes clung to her skin.

Emerging from the tent, she stretched out the kinks in her body that had accumulated through the night. During the first few weeks on the trail, she'd been covered with bruises from sleeping on the hard ground with only a few thin blankets to pad the rocks. Over time she'd become accustomed to the hard bed and even bugs that crept beneath the blankets. Occasionally a mouse or rat would sneak in and then they'd have a lively party chasing it out. *Amazing what a body can deal with.*

As always, Mother was already awake and tending to the fire. She was a restless soul, not one for much sleep. Through the night, Ellie would hear her tossing and turning in the tent she shared with the little boys. She'd sit up every half hour to check her sons' breathing, and often she paced outside the tents as well, watching for varmints and Indians and heaven knew what else. She'd been lucky not to get shot by a night guard on accident. Some of the fellows could be nervous, trigger-happy sorts.

Ellie pulled her collecting basket from the wagon. "I'm going for chips," she called.

"Glory be. Thank you." Mother wiped her hands on her apron. "I just threw the last one in the fire."

Ellie started out past the circle of wagons. Grazing oxen and horses lifted their heads to stare at her as she ambled by. Other women and children fanned out with their own baskets and buckets.

Buffalo chips were scarce here, and the endless stream of wagons had picked much of the area clean. Ellie was forced to go quite a distance from camp to find the day's ration. Good thing they'd had no reports of Shoshone raiding parties lately. Still, she dared not wander too far.

She picked up a few crumbling pieces, giggling at the absurdity of the situation. *I never thought I'd be searching for cow patties with such urgency.* Her father was a shopkeeper, and they lived in town.

The family hadn't owned a cow, or even chickens, until they'd left for Oregon.

Ellie's grandfather had been a farmer, and Father always dreamed of owning his own land. After years of discussing the idea until it became an obsession, he'd come home one night and announced they'd received permission to claim their own fifty-acre block of land in the Willamette Valley.

The color had drained from Mother's face as she'd clutched Heston, then a newborn, to her chest. "Tom, this is madness," she'd gasped. "The war ended last year, with a possible resurgence. Johnny Rebs might still hide out in the wilderness, waiting to rob folks. Not to mention sicknesses, and Indians."

"It's the will of God," Father had said firmly. "I've already spoken to Harvey Winkins. He's wanted my store for years and he'll pay me cash for the inventory we don't take along to Oregon with us." A slow smile had spread over his face. "Our destiny awaits, Martha, my love. The children will run through the woods and learn to raise crops, like I did. A healthier life we cannot find."

"How can we make such a dangerous journey?" Mother had covered her face with her free hand. "We have the younger boys, and this one." She'd gestured to the new baby, who gurgled and cooed.

"Won't be easy, Martha. I'd never say that. We'll make it."

Father had gotten his way, as always. The wagons had been purchased and filled, essential items packed, and any non-vital possessions sold.

A month before the family planned to leave, Ellie had come down with scarlet fever. For her, those weeks were filled with shadow and heat, shut up in a room away from her siblings to keep them from the dreaded sickness.

When she'd returned to a state of lucidity, Father had departed, along with her two oldest brothers, Robert and Johnny. They'd been forced to go ahead or lose the land they'd claimed.

She hadn't even been able to say goodbye.

A year later, Ellie had regained part of her strength and Heston could toddle for short distances. Her mother sold their home, and the rest of the family started on the trip to Oregon. Ami, a friend of the family, came along to help with the children. Two men, Tad and Burt, were hired to drive the oxen.

And now Ellie scavenged for buffalo chips.

She moved faster, studying the ground with a trained eye, checking for any that could be half-buried or covered with grass. Sometimes grass grew brighter and greener above larger clumps.

Her basket was half-full now. She straightened and scanned the area.

An alcove of rocks shielded her from the sun and view of the other searchers. This wasn't the safest place to be, out of sight, but Ellie basked in the momentary solitude. She threw back her head and allowed the sun to warm her face, though too long and she'd risk her fair skin being scalded. Her lips parted, and before she could stop them, a song tumbled forth.

"New every morning is the love
Our wakening and uprising prove;
Through sleep and darkness safely brought,
Restored to life and power and thought.

New mercies, each returning day,
Hover around us while we pray;
New perils past, new sins forgiven . . ."

The notes died on her tongue as an impossible sound reached her ears. The sweet strains of a violin playing nearby, echoing off the rocks.

A smile spread across her face, and she peeked around the side of the bluff.

Thaddeus leaned against the wall, his head bare. Sun gleamed off his shining violin. His eyes were closed, and his bow danced along the strings of his instrument.

Ellie sang the last line of the chorus along with the violin.

"New thoughts of God, new hopes of Heaven."

Thaddeus set the violin to the side. "Good morning, song-bird. How's chip hunting?"

Ellie pulled herself back from the heavenly place she'd been, blinking a bit in the face of tangible reality. "A bit sparse," she admitted. "Are your sisters out searching?"

"Not today. My mother hates cooking over the stuff." He rubbed his chin. "It's useless to fret over such things if you ask me. I make my own fires now. If I eat one more can of cold oyster soup, I might drop dead right on the plains."

"Are you hunting for chips?" Ellie asked doubtfully, her eyes trained on the violin.

"No. I always do my chores before daylight. Then I find a place to play. It's my way of interpreting Psalms 108:2. "Awake, lute and harp! I will awaken the dawn," Thaddeus quoted.

This outburst didn't surprise Ellie. Thaddeus was always quoting scripture. He knew more Bible verses than anyone she'd ever met except for her pastor, back in Missouri. *And maybe even more than him.*

Thaddeus placed his fiddle on a springy patch of grass where it wouldn't slip. "Shall I help? I'm good at finding things."

Ellie grinned. "Skills so vital here. 'The finest chip hunters in the world!' Imagine what our classmates back home would consider such boastings."

Thaddeus laughed as he picked up bits of chips and dropped them into her basket. "I shudder to imagine. Like another land, isn't it?" He sobered. "Seems like a lifetime ago."

A question bubbled to Ellie's thoughts; one she'd wanted to ask for quite some time. "Why did you come on this journey, Thaddeus? You're a grown man. You could have stayed behind and gone to seminary."

Thaddeus straightened and stared out into the prairie. "The obvious choice. However, I felt the call of God to join my family, as silly as they can be at times. God has a destiny for me in Oregon, and I hope to find a church to lead there. He'll show me when it's time."

Ellie rested her chin in her hands.

"I'd love to minster to people who need help. I wanted to journey to the field tents during the war to help nurse the soldiers, but Mother wouldn't let me. Someday I'd like to help at an orphanage. Or preach to the Indians."

Thaddeus raised an eyebrow. "No shortage of folks in need."

"What could I do for them? I'm a young girl from a poor family."

"For starters, you could sing. You have a lovely voice, Ellie."

She stared down at the ground, her eyelashes fluttering against her cheeks. "I don't know if I could ever have the courage to sing in front of other people."

"I remember when I first prayed before a crowd. My lips trembled so badly I could scarcely form the words." Thaddeus rested his chin on steepled fingers. "I had to remind myself, it wasn't for me. I was speaking to God. Of course, Father didn't like it. He doesn't believe I should become a preacher."

Ellie bit her lip. "Doesn't the Bible say we should honor our parents?"

"Honor has nothing to do with bowing to unreasonable demands, especially when a body is of age." Thaddeus chucked a particularly large patty into the basket. "Will I treat my parents with love and respect? Yes. I cannot put their wishes above the call of the Almighty God."

Ellie tilted her head. "How do you know when God has called you to do something?"

"Now that's tricky to explain." Thaddeus brushed off his hands and picked up his violin. "Sometimes it's a bubbling feeling, here." He tapped his chest. "Sometimes it's a voice in my mind speaking words I didn't conjure on my own. I knew by the age of twelve I'd be a preacher."

"I might know what you mean," said Ellie. "When I was in school, some friends of mine wanted to play in a shed out behind the school, one with rotten boards in the walls. I said I wouldn't, and they called me chicken."

Thaddeus's eyes narrowed. "Why didn't you go?"

"The thought made me sick to my stomach," Ellie said. "My friends went anyway. . . and the building collapsed. No one died, but my best friend received a big gash on her head. Two other girls were hurt as well."

Thaddeus nodded. "Sounds as though the Holy Spirit was definitely speaking to you."

Ellie picked up the heaping basket. "Thanks for your help with the chips." She paused. "We baked bread in our skillets yesterday. Mother won't mind if I give your family some."

"My father wouldn't allow me to accept it."

Ellie pursed her lips. Her family's survival had depended, at times, on the kindness of neighbors. And her sweet, sturdy mother had done plenty of tending to friends when they were sick and helping out with the 'poor folks' as she called them. Ellie couldn't imagine a life where kindness was simply turned down. "You'll change your mind when you become a minister," she said. "All the ministers I knew were as poor as pittance."

"Laborers are worthy of their hire," Thaddeus said. "I'll do what is needed when I have a flock, Lord willing." He wiped his hands on his faded trousers. "Have a good day, songbird. I hope we can sing together again soon."

3

Poison Pool

Thaddeus gripped the wooden yoke and dug his heels into the dirt. The ox bellowed and rolled his eyes.

"Julep, I've told you a hundred times," Thaddeus said through clenched teeth. "Alkali pools are death. You want to end up with all those other critters?" He waved at the piles of yellowed bones that lined the path, along with rotted furniture, broken wagons, and grave markers made from every material imaginable, including clock faces and washing boards.

The gesture proved to be a mistake. The ox took advantage of the slack and pressed forward.

His yokemate, Crumble, fought against his plunging brother.

"See, listen to your partner! He knows what's better. Be patient. There's a fresh watering hole a mile up."

He shook his head and grinned, despite the dire situation. "Five months on the trail and my mind is addled, talking to oxen like they understand."

All through the wagon train, other drivers waged similar wars with their animals. On this section of trail, the poisonous pools were impossible to avoid. Each time they approached water after a long stretch of drought, the drivers employed all their strength and wits to avoid a stampede.

"How're you doing back there?" Thaddeus yelled.

James, the driver the Herschel family had employed, yelled back. "Brake's holding, but this wagon wheel is nearly gone."

The change in weather from blazing hot days, to freezing nights, along with weeks of constant rain earlier in the trip, had not been good for the schooners. Many of the wagons were shaky and unstable, threatening to break down completely and leave entire families stranded.

"Hopefully we'll find a replacement at Fort Bridger," said Thaddeus. "We should be there within three weeks."

"I don't know if the rim'll last," James shouted back.

Thaddeus sent up a prayer for extra strength as he fought the straining ox. From early childhood he'd shared all thoughts and feelings with the Lord. The idea that the Creator of heaven and earth could hear the deepest secrets of his mind had always been a source of fascination and comfort.

His father was an important banker. His family had enjoyed a life of wealth and comfort until they'd embarked on their westward journey. Though Thaddeus had always been expected to follow in his father's footsteps, he held a quiet hope that somehow he'd find a way to walk into his true calling. In a small way, he'd been able to do that on this journey. He led small Bible studies and prayers on Sundays, and he'd already officiated two weddings.

The bellows of the oxen grew louder, and Julep strained with all his might, his muscles rippling.

There it is. The calm lake, hundreds of yards across, laying like a white mirror. Not a ripple from a fish, nor so much as a tiny bug skated over the beautiful but deadly water.

A man shouted, and two mules thundered by, their harnesses dragging behind them.

Henry Blake. Thaddeus groaned. The Blake family had dealt with their share of misfortunes. Tangled as he was with his own oxen, he could only pray that the Blakes would catch their mules before too much water was consumed.

Mr. Herschel came up beside Thaddeus. "I'll take the other side," he said. "Crumble will do his work, like he always does."

The passing of the pool, a distance that should have been traversed in moments, took nearly half an hour. Between Thaddeus, Mr. Herschel, and Crumble, Julep was finally convinced to veer away to the safer path. Mercifully, this lake was smaller than most. One such place, a few days back, had taken hours to circle.

As the path straightened, Julep's stride became loose and ambling once more.

"I must check on your mother." Mr. Herschel let go of Crumble's yoke and disappeared behind the wagon.

Thaddeus relaxed his grip. "Francie, can you come take Julep's head?" he called. "I'm going back to make sure Jerusha is all right."

"I suppose." Francie came to his side. "This is my last dress that hasn't been stained or mended. I'll make the sacrifice."

Thaddeus rolled his eyes. How his sister could consider such things escaped him. Most of the women of the trail had dresses patched with flour sacks and bits of blanket. Except for his mother, of course, who rode in the wagon, and their younger sister, Maggie. They'd packed enough clothes for an army of women and bought whatever new dresses were offered in the sparse shops along the way.

He'd learned that arguing with the three women of his family never did any good. "Thank you, Francie. I'll return shortly."

He turned on his heel and threaded his way through the dozens of wagons.

Ellie stepped beside him, her hair, like braided sunshine, glowing through the dust. She smiled shyly. "Good morning, Thaddeus. I hope Julep is well?"

Thaddeus nodded. "Yes, we managed to keep the old codger from drinking his death. I am glad your family's beasts have the sense to keep away from the alkali."

She wrinkled her nose. "We're fine, but did you see Mr. Blake's mules?"

"Yep. Didn't know mules could run so fast with all those harnesses."

"One animal got in a few good swallows before they caught him. I'm heading to Jerusha's for a potion. She's saved other creatures with it."

"I'm going there myself, to check on her." Thaddeus tore his eyes away from Ellie's face, to avoid staring. Despite months on the trail, Ellie's eyes still held sparks of joy and life. She'd grown from waifish and frail to a strong, capable woman, always retaining her quiet beauty.

Several weeks had passed since Thaddeus and Ellie had first greeted the morning together with music. Thaddeus found himself forcing his eyelids open earlier each day, in hope they could meet again. When he found Ellie waiting for him, her pink cheeks and quick smile made him imagine she'd hurried for him too.

Many days the chores would be too numerous, and one of them wouldn't have a chance to steal away. Most days there'd be time enough for at least one hymn.

Somehow, they'd managed to keep these worship sessions a secret from the other members of the wagon train. Not that Thaddeus would have been embarrassed to be 'caught' singing for God. For some reason he longed to keep these sacred moments between him, God, and Ellie.

They reached Jerusha's wooden painted wagon. The old woman stood by her lead mule, rubbing the animal's trembling legs and speaking in comforting tones. Her pet crow, Archibald, was perched on her shoulder.

"How did Firefly do?" asked Ellie.

Jerusha straightened and rubbed her shoulder, sending Archibald squawking to the mule's back. "Hello, friends," she said. "Firefly did fairly, this time. Poor dear can't understand when I stop her from quenching her thirst. Safer waters lie ahead, but she doesn't know that."

"Our Julep is the same way," said Thaddeus, "else I'd have been here to help you."

Jerusha swatted a fly from the mule's ear. "We care for our own creatures on this journey first, and then help the neighbors beside us. I can manage my Firefly. She trusts me, though she doesn't always like what I have to say."

She gave the mule one last pat on her nose.

"Do you have any more of that cleansing draught?" Ellie asked. "Mr. Blake's mule broke away."

Jerusha chuckled. "I've told folks a dozen times it's simply quinine and bacon fat, which most people have in their own supplies. However, there's something magical about fetching it from a healer, isn't there?" She pulled her wagon's brake and opened the round wooden door on the side. "Plenty of bacon grease here. My quinine's low. Might have a drop or two left in the bottle to mix up. I'll have to put in for more when we reach the fort."

Thaddeus rolled his eyes. 'When we reach the fort' had been the constant chant for the last few days. These oases of refuge and supplies dotted the trail, but days, and sometimes weeks, of travel separated them.

Jerusha emerged with a small bucket, covered with cheesecloth. "Don't go opening that unless you want to unleash a stench upon the wagon train," she warned. "And say a prayer for the Turner family. Little June came down with a cold this morning. I fixed up some mulberry bark tea. She was quite weak." She stared down at her hands. "What folks need is a rest. Captain Marshall keeps pushing on. He's playing the Devil's panpipes, that man is."

"I'm sure we'll stay a day or two at the next good watering place. Or at least when we reach the fort," said Thaddeus.

"I hope so," Ellie said, with the wistful smile that always tempted Thaddeus to catch her up in his arms and offer her the world.

Jerusha glanced from his face to Ellie, and the side of her mouth quirked up.

Hopefully Jerusha is the only one who suspects my feelings. At least she'll keep my secret. Thaddeus stroked Firefly's nose one last time. "Are you sure you won't be needing us?"

"I was prepared for these tough stretches when I decided to come on this journey alone," Jerusha replied. "I have a long way to go. I hear the mountain passes are pretty rough."

Ellie shuddered. "I can't imagine worse terrain than the last group of hills. Especially when it started raining before all the wagons made it down the slope. I've never seen such mud."

Jerusha patted her shoulder. "God has brought more folks along this trail than a body can count. Otherwise the Willamette Valley would still be empty. We'll make it."

Ellie dipped her head. "I know. Sometimes I wish I could wake up and find myself there instead of having to go through it all."

"The butterfly can only fly if it struggles to emerge from its chrysalis," said Thaddeus.

Jerusha smiled. "Sounds like a good topic for your next sermon, my boy."

Thaddeus and Ellie returned to the front of the train. Ellie held the bucket close to keep it from sloshing.

"Would you like me to carry it for you?" asked Thaddeus.

"I can manage," said Ellie. "Thank you."

Ellie always seemed to act in a formal, polite manner when Thaddeus encountered her within the wagons. So different from the mornings when they were alone, singing together. Questions rose to his lips. He desperately wanted to ask why she acted like that. But perhaps he knew the answer.

Ellie's mother was deathly afraid for her oldest girl. The first few months on the trail she'd barely let her out of her sight. Thaddeus couldn't begin to imagine the fear that came from almost losing a child, but Ellie was a woman now. They'd celebrated her eighteenth birthday weeks before with peppermint sticks Francie had conjured up from somewhere.

He couldn't lose the stirring he felt whenever he thought of Ellie. She had a way of speaking to his soul, with her quiet observations, and her sweet, heartfelt songs. So much stood against them. How could they possibly have a future?

Thaddeus reached his wagon and waved to Ellie. "Let me know what happens with the mule."

"I will." She walked on, her golden braid swishing behind her.

Thaddeus hurried back to Julep and Crumble.

Hours later, a call flew through the wagon train. Fresh water had been sighted.

The train leaders led their animals to pull the first wagons into the circle formation. Older children took the free oxen, mules, and horses to the watering hole. This dance was performed every night– a dusty, grungy job necessary to keep the livestock hemmed in and the members of the train safe from dangerous animals and men.

Finally, the Herschel wagons were settled. Thaddeus unyoked Crumble and Julep and led them down to the small, cool spring, thankfully a dusky green instead of the eerie white alkali.

The oxen drank, their hollowed sides filling like the inflated pig bladders Thaddeus played with as a child.

"There's a good boy." Thaddeus patted Julep's flank.

The bright blue sky deepened to a soft purple, and evening peepers sang their song from their various spots in the pond. Grateful animals guzzled the fresh water greedily, and peace blanketed the camp.

4
Wheels and Smoke

"That's finished, at least." Ivy put her hands on her hips and surveyed the rolled-up tent. "Told you I could do it all by myself."

Ellie gave her younger sister a quick hug. "I couldn't have done it better."

Ivy beamed, her dimples flashing in the morning sunlight. As the middle child, Ivy was expected to do what she was asked and move along with the flow of the family. And this she did, but with a gusto that was often hard to ignore. She fought her way into the thick of things like a force of nature, never stirring up too much fuss, but always making sure her presence was known.

Ellie took the tent to the back of the wagon and stacked it neatly with the other two. How many times had she performed this task? The mundane morning drills. Clean up from camp, eat breakfast. Trudge for miles beside the oxen or spend time corralling her brothers, who seemed bent on self-destruction throughout the journey. They were all prisoners, though no bars and walls held them. The endless lands and merciless weather did that well enough.

A smile lit upon her lips. She would meet Thaddeus today. For a while, all would be bright and new, her soul's empty reservoir refilled.

"Good morning, girls." Mother handed them cold potatoes, baked in the coals the evening before. "Here's your breakfast. No time to cook today, Captain Marshall said we're heading out early. He wants to reach the fort as quickly as possible, so we can rest and prepare for the next mountain crossing."

Ellie groaned. So much for her plans to meet Thaddeus. She stuffed the potato in her apron pocket. Right now, the morsels would simply stick in her throat.

"Isn't it exciting?" Ivy clasped her hands together. "Soon we'll be up in the mountains and away from this eternal dust."

God, give me the optimism of that child. "Twill be a nice change," Ellie said, pulling her sister's sunbonnet over her eyes and tying the ribbons firmly under her chin. "You must keep a sharp eye on Heston. He almost flew over the ridge chasing after a butterfly on that last trek, and the mountains ahead will be harder."

The morning passed uneventfully, with Ellie minding the three boys for a spell. To the delight of all, they passed through a glorious riot of flowers, much bigger and brighter than the normal desert scrubs. Soon even the older women filled their arms with the lovely blossoms, inhaling deep breaths of the delicious fragrances, a welcome mask to sweat and mold.

Ellie stooped to pluck a glowing purple blossom that peeped, like a jewel, from beneath a currant bush. She tucked it into her braid, feeling for all the world like a queen.

"Lovely choice." Thaddeus walked up behind her. Despite his kind words, his mouth was drawn, and his shoulders slumped.

Ellie's heart gave a tiny skip like always when she saw Thaddeus. "Is everything all right?"

"I'd like to say yes." Thaddeus plunged his hands into his coat pockets. "But that would be a dreadful lie. Our wagon wheel hit a stone and has crumbled to rubble. We were prepared for a disaster like this, though we hoped it would hold on for a bit longer. The thing was hanging by a splinter. I'll have to ride ahead of the wagon train to the trading post and fetch a new one."

"That sounds dangerous." Ellie frowned. "Aren't we still quite a ride away?"

"A day by wagons, a few hours for a single rider. I'll have to take a mule to carry the wheel." Thaddeus rubbed the back of his neck. "We'll repair the wagon and ride through the night to catch up."

"Surely someone else has a spare wheel."

"Nope. I've ridden up and down asking," replied Thaddeus. "Everyone's stretched to their limit on wagon parts. Seems like half the schooners are barely hanging on, so to speak. Folks are praying the supply post will have enough supplies. We're putting a lot of hopes on the place if you ask me," he said in an uncharacteristically dark tone.

"Oh, Thaddeus, don't forget, God will take care of us," said Ellie. "Perhaps Captain Marshall will allow a delay."

"The wagons are stopping for lunch now," said Thaddeus. "I won't be back by the time the train starts again and Captain Marshall will not let them wait. He's anxious to reach fresh water for the beasts and I don't fault him for that. I'm not afraid for Father and myself. We can get the wheel and repair it without much trouble."

"Don't we still need to worry about Shoshone parties?"

"No word of any attacks like that for weeks." His brow furrowed. "I'm concerned for Mother. Her wagon lost the wheel. There's not room in the second wagon for a rider, and we don't have time to move all the supplies."

"Oh." Ellie stared at the ground. Mrs. Herschel had barely emerged from her wagon for weeks, and when she did, she tottered to the fire for a few moments, complained of 'vapors,' and returned to burrow beneath the stack of quilts and blankets Francie had told Ellie she mostly lived in. "That does sound bad."

Mother came to stand by Ellie's elbow. "This isn't a problem, Thaddeus. Your mother can join us for the day. We have room in one of our wagons since Ellie often rides with Heston."

Oh, Mother, no! Ellie wanted to protest. Having Mrs. Herschel in their wagon would be like caring for another child.

Thaddeus's cheek twitched, and his hands trembled.

Her defiance wilted. She could never say no to those pleading eyes. She rested a hand on his elbow. "Thaddeus, she should come with us."

Thaddeus's shoulders sagged. "That's generous of you, Ellie, Mrs. Davis. I'll talk to Mother and Father."

A half-hour later, Mrs. Herschel had been settled in the Davis wagon, amidst many protests and whimpers. Mr. Herschel stayed back with the broken wagon. The driver, James, Francie, and Maggie walked beside the supply schooner, along with the rest of the train.

Ellie watched as Thaddeus strapped the broken wheel to the back of his patient mule. "Is there no one else who can ride with you?"

"The Almighty and His angels." Thaddeus pushed his hat back and smiled. "If He's with me, I couldn't ask for a better companion."

Captain Marshall stomped over, his big boots creating mini dust clouds around him. "You've got yer compass, boy, but the path should lead you right there. Should get to the fort in a few hours. Don't linger, and you'll be back by dark. Told yer father he'll have to clean out most items to make the wagon lighter as ta' catch up." He mopped sweat off his bald, shining forehead. "I hate to leave your father here by hisself. No men could be spared."

"I understand, sir." Thaddeus clasped his hand. "Don't fret for us. There'll be another train coming by, perhaps today. They might assist with the wheel, otherwise, we'll manage. We should see you all by tomorrow night."

Francie and Maggie tearfully hugged their brother. Ellie wanted to do the same but knew the gesture would hardly be proper. Instead, she waited until no one was watching, and pushed her handkerchief in his hand. "To hold my prayers," she whispered.

"Thank you." Thaddeus stared down at her, his eyes searching her face, his mouth quivering. He tucked the lacy bit of cloth into his breast pocket, mounted his horse, and rode away.

Thaddeus whistled a hymn, and his fingers itched for his fiddle. Flowers thickened beneath Ol' Ben's hooves, until the horse appeared to be wading through a rainbow, flattened stalks marking the path behind them. The day couldn't have been more beautiful, with the sun's blazes tempered by a mountain breeze.

If only Ellie were here. She'd ride behind him, her arms tight around his midsection. He'd feel her sweet breath on his back, and they could sing all the way to the wagon.

Silly Thaddeus. A trip like that and they'd both ruin their reputations for life. *Not if we were married.* He allowed himself to fall into a hazy dreamland where Ellie was queen.

The mule stomped along placidly, water still dripping from her muzzle. The fort had been built beside a cool river, and Thaddeus was gladdened to know the folks of the wagon train would soon arrive in the presence of good food and fresh water. *Perhaps we'll have time to fish. Captain Marshall told us we'd stay at the fort a few days to gear up for the mountain pass.*

He'd taken a differing route, one quicker for a horse and a mule. As he stopped for a mouthful of hard tack, he spotted the wagon train a distance away. He considered riding up for a quick hello but decided against it. Though his sisters and mother would've been sore glad to see him, greetings and lamentations would eat up more of his time.

As he moved on, there was no sign of varmints running through the grass, and even flies and mosquitoes had seemed to take their business elsewhere. He shielded his eyes and scanned the prairie. Another mile or so and he'd reach his father and the wagon.

A plume of smoke greeted his gaze. *Too high. Too wide.* He clicked to his horse and dug in his heels. The mule behind him grunted, reminding him of her extra burden. *The wagon wheel.* He reined his horse in a bit, slow enough for the mule to keep up with a dismal trot.

The smell of smoke intensified, not the friendly aroma of a cozy campfire, but the acrid stench of ruin and death.

He drew closer to a dark patch in the grass, his heart pulsing until he thought it might burst. The blackened, smoldering ribs of a wagon met his eyes, and an invisible fist gripped his throat. His family's schooner. *It must be.*

Mechanically, he dismounted and stumbled forward, fear slamming him in fresh, unfettered waves. "Father? Father!"

A bloodied brown waistcoat and a battered straw hat lay scattered in the grass, and past them, a man. Thaddeus ran to the inert body and turned him face up. "Father!" he shouted.

His father's eyes were swollen shut, and a trickle of blood ran from his nose. "Looters," he groaned through cracked lips.

A sharp pain slammed into Thaddeus's chest. "You're alive! Oh, Father, why did we leave you! I came back as quickly as I could."

His father stared up at him through slitted lids. "Son. Nice to see you." He tried to prop himself up on an elbow but fell back. "They took everything in the wagon. All our supplies." He cracked a smile and winced. "Good thing your mother traded out her best treasures for vittles, eh? And they didn't get the gold. It's in the other wagon."

"How long ago?" A desire for vengeance filled Thaddeus, an overwhelming fury he'd never felt before.

"Hours? I don't know, son. I've been laying here, letting the bugs crawl over me." His father grimaced. "They beat me up pretty bad. I believe the one would have killed me, but the other told him not to waste his bullets. They wore bandannas so I wouldn't recognize them."

Thaddeus took a few deep breaths, willing away the white hate that filled his soul. "Where does it hurt the most?" He unbuttoned his father's shirt as gently as possible, wishing very much that Jerusha was there.

"Here, mostly." His father touched his right side.

Thaddeus gently moved the leathered hand, the same hand that had taught him to write his numbers at the age of five, the same hand that had held his own when they walked through town together as a young child. A sickly red bruise was already forming, the edges already tinged with purple and blue. Smaller bruises clustered around it. He prodded the area gently, trying to ignore his father's groans.

"I don't believe any bones are broken. We'll have to get you to Jerusha to make sure." Thaddeus closed his eyes. *I can't go after these men. You will have to find justice for them, Lord.* He peered down at his father. "Thank the Lord there weren't any big gashes, you might have bled out."

"I'm not too happy with the Almighty right now," said his father.

Thaddeus clenched his fists. "I'm pretty angry myself, and I can see why you'd say that, Father. You're in pain. However, you could be dead. We lost one wagon. What if our whole family had stayed back? The girls could have been killed. The gold has been a worry from the trail's beginning, thank God we didn't lose that. Let's get you back to the wagon train."

His father closed his eyes. "It hurts to argue. You'd better help up me on that mule, Son, before I'm too stiff to move."

During certain hard times in Thaddeus's life, he'd been tempted to step away and let someone else do the hard work. As the only son, he'd been expected to help with whatever dirty, smelly job needed to be done, even at home when they'd had servants. His father said these tasks built character, and Thaddeus had to admit, they probably did. Still, never in his life had he wished more for someone, anyone–except for the bandits, of course–to come along, give a reassuring, "Step out of the way, son, we'll figure this out for you," and take care of matters.

He shielded his eyes and checked back over the path. No dust cloud to mark approaching schooners. The train following the closest was probably still several hours back, maybe even a day. And the looters might decide to return and finish the job . . .

Removing his shirt, he wrapped his father's chest, binding the sleeves tight over his heart. "This will help hold you together if you've broken a rib. Not sure what else I can do.'

His father gritted his teeth and nodded. "Probably best."

Thaddeus pulled out his knife and hacked the now unneeded wagon wheel free from ropes that tied it to the mule's pack. He kicked it to the side of the trail. "Maybe someone will find it and make use of it."

He surveyed the horse and mule. "Ben has the smoothest gait. I'll ride Bessie." He gulped as he thought of the proud, strong oxen they'd lost to the raiders. Those four beasts had taken them safely through the territory without faltering. *Hope the raiders treat them better than they treated Father.*

He led his horse to where his father lay. "There's no gentle way to do this. You'll have to get in the saddle somehow. I'll do my best to help you."

His father grimaced. "We'll both do our best, son."

Somehow, between Thaddeus and Ol' Ben, they managed to get the injured man on the horse and strapped in soundly with ends of ropes Thaddeus had used for the wagon wheel.

"I'll lead the horse, that way you can use all your strength to hold on," said Thaddeus.

His father didn't reply, just set his mouth in a thin line and stared ahead. Beads of sweat travelled down his face in crooked lines, but he didn't raise a hand to wipe them away.

As they moved along the trail, Thaddeus struggled for words. For much of his life he'd dreamed of being a pastor. Many of the pamphlets and studies he'd read stressed the importance of encouragement. "A merry heart doeth good like a medicine." But all he could focus on were the hot flashes of anger shooting through his own brain.

He'd encountered this part of himself enough to know that nothing good would come from feeding the beast. Every time a surge rushed past, he'd send it to the Lord. *Please, God. Help me. Help me to give this to you.*

How could they make the remaining ten-week journey to the Willamette Valley with only one wagon and two thirds of their oxen? *If only another man could have stayed behind with Father. If only I'd come back sooner. It might at least have been a fair fight. We might have saved the wagon.*

God didn't work in might-have-beens. He straightened. He could be mourning his father this moment, but his life was spared. *This will pass.* On the wagon train, his family was surrounded by friends. People who would give their last spoonful of beans to someone less fortunate. Despite the chest of gold his father had hidden in the other wagon, his family would fall into the 'needy' category they so despised. This was a trial of his faith, and he would endure.

5
Bluffs and Butterflies

Ellie wiped her face with her apron and scooped the last bit of porridge, garnished by the currants that seemed to grow throughout this green valley, into a bowl. Heston took the food, gave her a giant grin, and joined his brothers as they ate by the fire. Heston had only recently figured out how to serve himself with a spoon, and he was proud of his accomplishment, though much of the precious food still ended up on his face and hair. He was a favorite of the camp dogs, who visited often to check for scraps.

Loud wails continued to emerge from the Davis family wagon. Ellie rolled her eyes and winced. The seed of a headache had sprouted earlier that morning and was now fully grown, thumping through her skull.

Francie had been in the wagon with Mrs. Herschel ever since Thaddeus and Mr. Herschel returned that afternoon. Thaddeus with news of their wagon's grim fate, and Mr. Herschel more dead than alive. Thaddeus took Mr. Herschel off to Jerusha for doctoring and left Francie and Maggie to deal with their mother.

Mother settled next to Ellie and picked up her porridge. "And I thought Miss Ami started out spoiled," she said in a low tone. "I can't say I've met a more frazzled and bedraggled soul than that woman in there."

"We may have to get used to her," Ellie replied. "Captain Marshall already enquired at the fort. There's not a spare wagon or ox to be had for love or money, and we've weeks of travel before we reach Fort Hall."

Mother's face blanched. "Surely she can walk beside the wagon once we break camp."

"She hasn't so far, according to Francie." Ellie rolled the last currant around her tongue, savoring the tart sweetness. "Not for a single day."

Mother blew out a gusty sigh that seemed to encompass the entire trip to Oregon thus far. "We must make the best of the situation. We can't turn out a neighbor."

Ellie felt a change in subject was prudent. "Did anyone check at the fort for mail?"

"Not a scrap." Mother spread out her leathered, berry-stained hands. "I was hoping to get a letter from your pa by now. Terrible things keep stirring up in my mind. A word from him would sure ease my fears." Her mouth drew down at the corners. "What if we arrive and no one's there? Or three graves . . . "

"Oh, Mother." Ellie pressed her hand against her heart. "Don't even suggest such calamity. They'll be fine. Really, they're safer than we are out here on the trail."

Mother blinked. "You're right. I will not allow my tongue to bring bad luck upon us all."

Ellie glanced at Ivy and the boys, who were now watching her and Mother with wide, bright eyes.

"Pa's all right, isn't he?" said Dan, the chronic worrier, even at five.

Mother brushed a bright tear from the corner of her eye, rose and smiled quickly. "Of course he is. Right as rain. And Robert and Johnny right along with him. They're probably talking about us right now. They're fixing up our rooms and putting up crops so when winter comes along, we'll be cozy as lightning bugs and have food to eat a'plenty. It is Oregon, after all."

"Will there be molasses for our johnnycake?" Dave said wistfully.

Ellie picked him up and swung him around, as though he were Heston's age again. "Molasses and raisins and . . . Dave, I hear they have cherries."

The children gasped.

"Cherry pie!" Ivy squealed.

"Hello." Thaddeus stood at the edge of the fire.

Ellie placed the still giggling Dave back on the ground, straightened, and patted a stray tendril of hair into place. "Good morning, Thaddeus. How is your father?"

A dark shadow flickered over Thaddeus's face, but he forced it back with the corners of his upturned mouth. "Jerusha says he'll mend, thank the Almighty. His ribs were only badly bruised, not broken."

"That's a relief," said Mother. "What cruel men could hurt a defenseless soul?" She shook her head. "And we've been worried about the Shoshone."

Thaddeus rubbed the back of his neck. "Between this and Miss Ami being kidnapped by the bounty hunters, the worst folks we've encountered on this journey have been white."

Another wail floated out from the Davis wagon. Two bright spots bloomed on Thaddeus's cheeks. "I'd better go see if I can help Francie. With Mother, the tiniest event can bring on a fit of vapors, so I can't imagine what all of this has done to her. Perhaps I can convince her to go with Francie and Maggie to the fort. Maybe a new hat will help her feel better." He gave a small smile. "That's what Father always did back home. I saw one in the window of the dry goods store. Pretty dusty, but it had an ostrich plume the size of my arm. Might lift her spirits."

"The fresh air can't hurt." Mother's tone was cheerful, but she darted Ellie a look that spoke a mouthful. Ellie knew she was wondering what they would do if Mrs. Herschel insisted on riding in their wagon all the way to Oregon.

As if reading her thoughts, Thaddeus doffed his hat and ran his hands through his thick dark hair. "Mrs. Davis, we'll clear what we can from our remaining wagon. Providential this all happened here. We can sell items in town and trade for food. My mother will have to walk like the rest of us."

"What if she don't want to?" asked Dan,

"Dan!" Mother chided. "Children should be seen and not heard."

Dan wrinkled his nose. "Then how will I know anything?"

Thaddeus patted Dan on the head. "We'll figure it out. Until then," he held out a gold coin to Mother. "Father wanted me to give you this for your trouble and the food you've provided."

Mother stared at the coin, her mouth in a thin, stubborn line that Ellie knew well. "Don't need the money, Thaddeus, thank you anyways. If you can do some hunting while we're camped in this valley, fresh meat would be a blessing. My drivers will be looking as well, so maybe between the lot of you we'll get lucky."

Lucky. That word again. Always with the luck.

Thaddeus returned the coin to his pocket. "All right, I can do that. I plan to hunt tonight before dusk, if all is settled with my father and mother. A valley this green ought to at least have some rabbits, if the settlers and soldiers haven't hunted it out."

He ducked into the wagon, and Francie emerged.

Francie's hair was in more dishevelment than Ellie had seen since they'd started for Oregon, even in the worst of the rain and dust. Dark rings rimmed her eyes and she looked as though she'd aged ten years in the last night.

"Is everything all right?" Ellie asked in a low voice.

"No. Everything is not all right," Francie replied in a stiff tone. She dabbed at the corners of her eyes. "It's wicked to say, with Father having his life and the gold–the most important items not being stolen." She clenched her fists, and her eyes narrowed. "This trip has been worse than the fires of Hades, and I hate Father for making us come."

Ellie's mouth dropped open, but Mother held out her arms.

Francie flew into Mother's embrace, unleashing a torrent of tears. "Why did we come? Oh why, oh why did we come? We could be safe in Memphis right now, in our beautiful home with a bath and beds and clean sheets. My father is an evil, greedy man!"

Mother stared over the sobbing girl's head and made a motion to shoo all the children away.

"Come now, let's go dig for worms." Ellie beckoned for her brothers to follow. "I hear the river is hopping with fish."

Wake the song of jubilee,
Let it echo o'er the sea!
Now is come the promised hour,
Jesus reigns with sov'reign pow'r

The last strains of the violin rang out over the mountain, and Ellie clasped her hands. "Oh, Thaddeus, it sounds so lovely here on the bluff. It makes me almost wish the full length of our journey was through the mountains."

Thaddeus dropped the bow to his side and made a face. "If I could go my entire life without bracing a wagon down a steep hill again, I'd be a happy man. But I know what you mean. It is beautiful."

Ellie hugged herself against the morning chill that had set in the last few days since they'd started the Bear Mountain path. The landscape fanned out before them, in reds and greens and browns, like a woven Indian blanket, with boulders dotting the terrain like tiny beads, though in reality they could crush entire towns if dropped from the sky. Eagles and hawks swooped lazily on the wind currents, barely bothering to flap their magnificent wings.

"I'd be happy to live on the side of a hill for always." Ellie swept her arm out. "It'd make me feel like an angel."

Thaddeus stared at her, a light shining in his eyes that she'd just begun to notice. "You sure are pretty enough to be one."

"Th–thank you." Ellie's cheeks warmed, though she'd been paid compliments before. Sometimes people in the street back home would reach out to touch her bright blond braid. The words felt different when they came from Thaddeus.

Suddenly, the feelings budding within her ever since she'd seen Thaddeus that first day on the trail bloomed to a full-blown rose. *I love Thaddeus. I will love him until the day I die.*

Thaddeus had ducked his head, a pink tinge creeping up his neck. "I'd better get back. Pa's doing better today, but I don't want him to take on too much since I'm not there."

Ellie nodded. They'd traversed the mountain path for three days after camping in the valley for a week. While the rest had been good for Mr. Herschel, Jerusha had warned him not to tire himself. Ellie frowned. A body would figure Thaddeus's mother had been the one attacked by bandits, considering all her hollering and wailing since the family had lost their wagon. Mr. Herschel had been compelled to rise from his sick bed and command his wife not to force her way back into the Davis wagon at the beginning of the journey up the mountains.

"We cannot push their oxen to strain so. Most belongings will have to be hauled up and down the steepest hills by hand. You know this, Betty."

"My nerves. They've never been this horrible!" Mrs. Herschel had sobbed.

Mr. Herschel finally coaxed her to their remaining wagon. Francie and Maggie followed, avoiding the stares of half the camp, who'd gathered to view the commotion.

Not for the first time, Ellie had been thankful her mother wasn't prone to theatrics and vapors. Mother had embarrassed her a time or two, but nothing like Mrs. Herschel.

Thaddeus led the way down the hidden path they'd discovered, offering a steadying hand over the worst of the rocks.

When Ellie grasped his hand, a tiny thrill rushed through her skin all the way to her soul. She'd had her share of schoolgirl crushes, mainly Bobby Quinlet, to whom she'd composed numerous poems on scraps of packing paper. This was a different sensation altogether. A wild, yet wholesome discovery that felt composed of all things true and bright and beautiful in the world. *Does he feel the same way?*

She attempted light conversation, pointing out a butterfly here, an unusual bush there, but Thaddeus gave short, absentminded replies. Obviously, his family issues were too pressing for him to notice the change in her demeanor. *For the best.* She should take time to mull over these feelings before sharing them. Another part of her ached to express her love.

It's not proper, she chided herself. *A man should be the one to speak his intentions first. Be patient, Ellie. If his feelings are true, he'll tell you when the time is right.*

Later that night, Ellie lay awake in her tent pondering the thought. *Would it matter if he did love me?* Their stations in life were so different. She was the daughter of a poor farmer. He was the son of a rich banker. Neither set of parents would approve of such a match, and when the wagon train reached Oregon, she and Thaddeus would have no prospects for setting out on their own. Perhaps after a year or two . . . but she could scarcely ask Thaddeus to wait for her that long. He was older than her by five years. He'd be ready to find a wife and start a family right away. Wasn't that the way most men were?

A tear trickled down the side of her face. Back home, the money part wouldn't have been such a problem. The Davis family home had been reasonable, and her parents always had what her mother called a 'tidy sum' in the bank. Her father was a successful shopkeeper with the busiest dry goods store in town. The family had sold most of their possessions, including her mother's family home, for their Oregon dream. On the other hand, though she and Thaddeus had grown up in the same town, she'd never met him or his family. They might never have even exchanged a glance if they hadn't ended up on the wagon train together. Truly, she couldn't fathom life without Thaddeus.

Finally, exhaustion won out over the struggles of her mind, and she drifted into a restless slumber.

6

Every Belonging

The morning dawned a dreary gray, but Ellie would not let it ruin her mood. She hummed a tune as she scrubbed out the water buckets from mold and scum that formed over night, even with the cold.

Her siblings tottered around the camp, rubbing bleary eyes. The cold nights were taking a toll on their sleep, though her mother had spent five dollars on two wool blankets from the fort. From what they heard, the rest of the journey would only be colder, especially as they ascended into the mountain passes. Dan and Dave went barefooted since they'd outgrown their shoes. Ellie shook her head. Hopefully, they'd find Indians with moccasins to trade.

With the buckets clean, she began the morning ritual. Only a few other people headed to the mountain spring for water this early, in the vague dawn light before the sun had peeped over the ridge.

Most of the wagon train had been looking forward to Soda Springs for months. They'd heard of the strangely colored red, gray and white bluffs, and the smooth gray rocks that looked as though they'd been hurled from another land.

The night before, most of the settlers had taken bathed in the warm waters of the springs, first the women, and then the men. They stood in awe to watch geysers shoot straight from the ground, some up to three feet high. A few of the men had sipped water from beer springs, and agreed it tasted like its namesake, to the shock of their wives. For the rest of the night, young boys were caught periodically sneaking off with cups and bowls to taste the 'whiskey water' for themselves.

Ellie reached the banks of the spring. She climbed to a high place on the bluff to catch the freshest stream of water as it gurgled from the rocks. Her muscles protested at the unfamiliar movements when she stretched to reach handholds, Still, the desire to be in a higher place urged her forward.

An overhang shielded a stone shelf from prying eyes. Ellie half expected Thaddeus to be waiting for her, violin in hand.

Instead, as she crept over the ledge, sniffles rang through the rocks, followed by stifled sobs. *Should I disturb them?* She paused. *What if they're hurt and need help?*

She inched around the shelf until she saw a girl, huddled against the stone wall.

"Francie?" she said.

Thaddeus's sister lifted her head. Tears streaked through the dust on her cheeks. She hastily wiped her face with the corner of her apron.

"What on earth?" Ellie placed her bucket on the shelf and edged closer.

"Oh, don't bother with me." Francie gave her a watery smile. "It's been a rough morning and I needed a teensy cry, is all."

Ellie scooted beside her and dangled her legs over the edge. "Is your father worse?"

"No, he's better." Francie wrung her hands. "I'm an ungrateful, wicked girl is what I am. I should be thankful that God spared his life. Where would we be if he hadn't been saved? No, I can't bear to tell you why I'm upset." She covered her eyes.

"Well, you don't have to say." Ellie ran her finger along the cool stone wall, enjoying its smoothness against her skin.

"No, I'll tell you." Francie's gray-blue eyes hardened like steel. "I'm sad because the few beautiful things I owned were in that wagon. My trunk with my favorite dress, the one I wore to our ladies' society social right before we left home. A darling hat made of snippets of straw with a veil. And my shoes. My last good white kid leather pair with twenty-seven black buttons on each side. They were cunning, those shoes, and there's small chance I'll find anything like them pair in Oregon."

"It's understandable that you're upset," said Ellie. "I have a hatbox like that. One pair of nice gloves, not that I wore them much at home, only to church. Two embroidered handkerchiefs my grandmother left me when she died. And a tortoiseshell comb given to me by Ami." A pain hit her chest. The thought of losing those precious, paltry items was enough to bring tears to her own eyes.

"It's not like I'm going to have a place to wear them again." Francie spit out the bitter words. "We'll be near a town, sure. I'd bet they don't have so much as a ladies' society there. Maybe the women in Oregon stay huddled in their homes, hidden away from all the dangers of the west."

Ellie tapped her chin. "I doubt that. Most of the women in Oregon have made the same trip we're making. And the ones born there will hear their mother's stories. Or their grandmother's. They're made of sturdier stuff than that. I'd bet their ladies' societies are wonderful."

"Maybe," Francie said. "And I suppose . . . if they don't have one already . . . Maggie and I could start one of our own?"

"Of course you can," said Ellie. "Why not?"

Francie took her hand. "It's lovely to have someone to talk to. Thaddeus would consider me shallow, even if he's too kind to say so. Maggie can't empathize. Little goose moved her things to the other wagon before we left."

"Well, that was fortuitous of her."

"For being so silly most of the time, she has remarkable perception." Francie gave a quavering laugh and wiped her eyes. "Thank you for listening. You're a good friend, Ellie."

Ellie blinked. She'd never really thought of Francie as a friend. She supposed that's what they had become, if only because they were the only unmarried women of their age on the wagon train. "You're welcome," she replied. "I know you'd do the same for me."

Francie pursed her lips. "Of course I would."

A long, loud whistle shrieked through the air. Ellie and Francie glanced at each other.

"The steamboat springs. Isn't it strange?" said Francie.

"I've never heard the like," Ellie said. "That noise is sure to wake the folks who are still sleeping." She peered over the embankment. "We ought to go back before someone tattles to our mothers. I'd rather not have a lecture for breakfast."

Francie stretched and crawled to the end of the ledge. "For all she worries about herself, my mother doesn't give a hoot what I do, as long as it doesn't inconvenience her or hurt the Herschel name."

Would I rather have a mother who worries too much? Or a mother who doesn't care at all? Ellie pondered this as they crept back down the edge of the embankment, and still hadn't decided when her feet hit the safe, solid rock below.

Thaddeus stared down at his mother's red, tearstained face, holding back the words of frustration that threatened to spew forth.

His mother clutched a small curio shelf in her spindly arms as though it were a beloved child. She squatted on a small pile of clothing and scattered items of furniture, glaring at anyone who dared approach her and these possessions.

The three Paiute natives who had come to barter stood in a cluster, speaking quietly in their own tongue. The food, hides, moccasins, and blankets they'd brought to trade were scattered at their feet.

"Betty, we must sell what we don't need for survival," Mr. Herschel said in a low, gentle voice. "The ice was an inch thick on our water pail this morning. Winter is coming, and we still have many mountains to cross. We're down to the last of our supplies, and Fort Hall didn't have much for us."

Thaddeus wanted to remind his mother that Fort Hall was two days behind them, and Fort Boise was nearly a month away, but he remained silent. These last several weeks on the trail had been the most miserable, and his mother impossible to reason with.

Francie came and placed a trembling hand on her mother's shoulder. "We've had to carry these items up and down each mountain, Mother. Maggie and I are worn to unravelling. Let's trade our trinkets for provisions."

Thaddeus's mother jerked away and rose from her hoard, a dangerous, manic glint in her eye that Thaddeus had never seen before. "Trinkets!" she cried. "This is not a trinket!" she held out the shelf. "This belonged to my mother, and her mother before. It's a precious, priceless heirloom and I won't sell it to a bunch of filthy savages!"

"Now, Betty, you want to ride in the wagon," Thaddeus's father said in a gentle, soothing tone. "If we trade these items, you'll have room to sit in the schooner again, at least for short stretches."

"I could ride now," Mrs. Herschel hissed, shaking Francie's hand from her shoulder, "if it weren't for that selfish Davis woman."

Thaddeus groaned. The Davis family needed the room in their wagon for the youngest child, who still couldn't toddle along for long distances. And for Ellie, who sometimes needed the rest, though she grew ever stronger. Whatever the reason, it didn't really matter. They had the right to reclaim their own space.

Though his mother owned two perfectly good feet and could more than keep up with the daily crawl, his sisters had been forced to coax her along, sometimes almost dragging her through the deep wagon ruts.

He glanced over his shoulder. Hopefully no one from the Davis family was close enough to hear his mother's embittered words.

His father pulled the curio from his mother's clutches with gentle fingers. "Let go, Betty. I'll buy you a nicer one when we reach our new home."

"It won't be the same!" Thaddeus's mother screeched. Her fingernails dug into the wood as his father pried it from her fingers.

Thaddeus took the item from his father and handed it to one of the natives, who nodded grimly.

"Nothing will ever be the same!" Thaddeus's mother leaned against his father's chest, her shoulders heaving with deep, racking sobs.

Mr. Herschel led his wife away.

Thaddeus hastily helped the Indians load the promised items onto their horses.

The Paiutes' mouths remained in solid, emotionless lines. Thaddeus was thankful. He didn't believe he could handle any sort of mockery made of his mother, though she might deserve it.

These men probably see this every day. Folks having to part with their dearest treasures, to survive this last stretch.

He joined the other members of the wagon train, collecting the goods they'd traded for.

Francie and Maggie came forward to help him. Francie's cheeks were flaming, and she wouldn't meet his eye. Thaddeus sensed she was as mortified, if not more so, than he was. Though Francie hadn't wanted to come on this trip, he'd been amazed at the quiet strength he'd shown through this experience, rarely complaining, always giving a quick smile. *Sometimes God uses trials to bring out the best in people.* His mother's bitter face rose in his thoughts. *Sometimes they bring out the worst.*

Jerusha hurried by, her hands empty.

"Did you make any trades, Miss Jerusha?" Maggie asked.

"I've had no chance, child," replied Jerusha. "I've been at the Davis wagon for hours. One of the girls has the fever."

Thaddeus's blood ran cold. "Is Ellie sick?" he managed to croak.

Furrows deepened on her forehead. "No, the younger one, Ivy. This train has entered a dark day. Four people have already been struck by this illness. Might have caught it at Fort Hall. There's no telling." She pursed her lips. "We must give our deepest prayers for

God's protection. These chill mountain winds don't bode well for the constitution."

"Is there a chance Ellie could still fall ill?" Thaddeus couldn't keep the edge of fear from his voice.

Jerusha nodded grimly. "We could all catch it, including you. We must all watch for symptoms. And I hate to say this, boy, but you'll probably need to sharpen up on your funeral sermon."

Thaddeus took his armload of supplies to the wagon, worry piling up on his shoulders like an invisible mound of rocks. He'd managed to get by without having to preside over the dead for this whole journey, though there'd been a few close calls. *Lord protect Ivy. Protect us all.*

7
Fever

The tent, though in the rare shade of a bluff, filled with compressed heat like a dutch oven with the lid tightened. Ellie dipped a rag in a basin and wiped the worst of the sweat from Ivy's forehead, only for the thick beads to return in an instant.

Ivy's closed eyelids twitched, and she muttered fitfully. Her breaths, deep and ragged, filled the walls. She rolled to the side and flung an arm over her face, as if to ward off the fever that had been tormenting her small body for the last week.

Heat and shadows. This sensation was all too familiar for Ellie, having been through her own dark days of scarlet fever a little over a year ago. These were her only memories from the dreadful time, along with her mother's cooling touch.

Twenty people were now affected by the fever in some form. Folks with mild cases still hobbled through camp doing chores, while the most ill hung in that precarious balance between this life and the world beyond. Two days ago, the wagons had been forced to stop in a thicket of trees beside a small stream. Black strips of cloth were tied at intervals along the trail to warn the trains behind them of the invisible dangers ahead.

Ellie pulled herself away from her sister and stepped outside the tent. "I'm off to get more tea from Jerusha," she called to her mother's bustling form, though she doubted she was heard. Mother had put herself in a constant state of business—her way of dealing with the worry and stress.

Next to their tents, a soft, crooning lullaby drifted through a canvas wagon cover. *Mrs. Martin.*

Felicity Martin, Maggie's dearest friend in the wagon train, was also sick.

As Ellie approached Jerusha's campsite, she heard voices.

"I don't think we have a choice, woman," came Captain Marshall's gruff tone. "I don't want to leave anyone behind, but if you've never crossed the Oregon mountain passes, you can't imagine the danger. If we wait even a few days, our journey could be lost."

Ellie stopped and ducked behind a tree. Though eavesdropping was shameful, this conversation seemed important.

"Seems to me, doctorin' is vital to all of you as well," came Jerusha's reply. "And I'm not leaving the sick folks. Besides. You don't look too well yourself."

"I'm fine," Captain Marshall blustered. "Stayed out in the sun too long yesterday. Get your hand away from my head."

"Like I thought, you're burning up," said Jerusha. "If I were you, I'd light a shuck to my wagon and get some rest."

Captain Marshall stomped past Ellie, so fast she had no time to pretend she wasn't listening. Thankfully, he didn't glance her direction, only muttered to himself.

Ellie scurried to the back of the wagon, where Jerusha was straining some evil-looking potion through a cheesecloth into a jar. Her deep blue dress was spattered with fresh orange and brown blotches, and her face was red from working in the heat, or perhaps her heated conversation.

Thaddeus hunched over a fire, stirring something in a large pot that hung from a chain over the flames. "Hello, Ellie." He straightened and stretched. "How's your sister?"

"The same." She gestured to the boiling cauldron. "What are you making?"

"Jerusha's showing me how to brew her fever tea," said Thaddeus. "I figured I'd be of some use over here since my folks are settled for the day. Shot a buck last night. The livestock is out grazing. Francie's with Maggie, who is beside herself with worry for Felicity."

"He's been a great help." Jerusha waved a piece of cheesecloth in his direction. "I tried to talk him into becoming my apprentice after this is all over, but he's not having it."

Ellie eyed the rows of small bottles beside Jerusha. "What do you call this sickness, Jerusha?"

Jerusha patted Archibald, who was, as usual, perched on her shoulder. "I'm not sure, though I've seen this fever before. It's not scarlet, and it's not influenza. No use quarantining folks, we've nowhere to put them."

"Some people are saying we caught the fever from the Indians," said Ellie.

Jerusha put a hand on her hip. "Much bigger chance it was brought on by the chill in the air, perhaps even an illness from the waters down at the fort. Leastways, it doesn't matter where it comes from, only that we can help those who ail from it."

"Will people die?" Ellie asked.

Jerusha kept silent. Her eyebrows knitted together and her mouth pressed into a grim line.

Will Ivy die? What would we do without Ivy? Ellie couldn't speak these words aloud. She grabbed a bottle of medicine. "How much for this?"

"Free for the taking. I'll not charge under the shadow of death," said Jerusha. "Shake it well and put a spoonful in a cup of hot water. Have Ivy drink as much as she'll swallow."

"Thank you." Ellie put the bottle in her pocket and rushed away.

"Ellie, wait." Thaddeus was behind her, the large apron he wore flapping around his knees. He caught up with her.

"I'm praying for your sister," he said.

"Do you think it will do any good?" she folded her arms tightly against her body.

"Of course I do," he said softly. "See that green slope over there?" He pointed to a hill several hundred yards from camp.

She nodded.

"Meet me there when you can."

"All right."

He headed back to Jerusha's wagon.

Ellie approached her sister's tent, shaking the bottle as she'd been instructed. Bracing herself for the stench of sickness, she went inside. Ivy lay exactly as she'd left her, jerking her head from side to side and murmuring unintelligible words.

Mother ducked in after Ellie and handed her a cup of steaming fish soup. "This is for you. You must keep your strength up or you'll be lying beside her." She nodded to Ivy. "I'll bring her some broth as well."

Dan poked his head under his mother's arm. "Will Ivy be all right, Mama?"

"With luck she will." Mother touched Ivy's thin shoulder under its heaping of quilts. "She's a strong fighter, our Ivy." Her eyes grew misty. "I've endured a fever with one daughter, I'll fight through it with another. And we'll pray that the rest of us are spared in this go-round."

Each morning, Ellie had woken with the cold fear of getting the fever herself. What would her mother do if more of them were stricken? What would they do if Mother were sickened herself? It was the fog they all stumbled through, with only hope to propel them forward.

Ellie left Ivy with her mother and slipped away to the hill Thaddeus had pointed out.

Across from the slope was an enormous bluff, where a waterfall thundered from hundreds of feet high. The water crashed and churned in white froth to the rocks below, a never-ending cacophony of sound. On most days, Ellie would have taken time to stop and marvel at this wonder, but now her soul was too heavy.

Thaddeus waited on a wide tree stump, grasses coming up to his boot tops. His head was lowered, and he did not glance up as she approached. His eyes were closed, lips moving in soundless prayer.

She scooted beside him on the stump and leaned her head on his shoulder. He put an arm around her, pulling her close. Instantly, love and comfort flowed through her soul, melting the stone walls she'd been constructing for the past week, ever since Ivy had been sickened.

Tears mixed with the prayers that poured from her spirit. She thought of Ivy, always tagging along, cheerful every day, always eager to help though sometimes it was more of a hindrance. They'd had an unspoken bond, being the only two girls. *She can't die. God, please don't let her die.*

She didn't know how long they were there, praying together. After a time, they both became silent and still. A breeze brought refreshing droplets from the waterfall to moisten their faces and necks.

Finally, Thaddeus spoke.

"God, we thank you for allowing us to bring our prayers before you. Thank you for sending your Holy Spirit to give us peace and rest. Thy will be done."

The morning wind whipped the women's hair about their shoulders, for most hadn't bothered to pin up their tresses or hide them under bonnets. Many of the men had mud on their shirts and hands, unwashed and unnoticed.

The group of people stood in a single line around six fresh mounds of earth.

Ellie stared at them. If she hadn't seen the muslin-wrapped bodies lowered in and covered, she would have a hard time believing that real people, folks she'd journeyed with for over four months now, had been placed inside. One was a child of seven. She sent a silent prayer of thanksgiving that God had spared Ivy, then felt instantly wicked for gloating in other folk's misery. An entire family of three, a couple and a young boy, had been taken from them yesterday. The other folks had passed in the last three days and had already been buried.

Captain Marshall, recovering but still shaky, stood at the head of the graves along with Thaddeus.

"We are here to mourn the loss of these fine people," Thaddeus said, extending his hand to the graves. "Let us remember where they are going. The Bible speaks of the beauty of Heaven. Wonders we can only dream of. Streets of gold. A crystal sea. A home prepared for us by a loving God, who sent his Son that all may have life."

Sniffles came from several places in the crowd, but many people smiled through their tears.

"We don't understand why God chooses to take some sooner than others. We can rest in the assurance that those who've given their lives to Him are waiting for us to join in the beautiful eternity."

He picked up his violin and began to play.

Abide with me; fast falls the eventide;
The darkness deepens; Lord, with me abide;
When other helpers fail and comforts flee,
Help of the helpless, oh, abide with me.
Swift to its close ebbs out life's little day;
Earth's joys grow dim, its glories pass away;
Change and decay in all around I see—
O Thou who changest not, abide with me.

As Ellie sang the sacred words, peace flowed through her, as it always did when Thaddeus played.

The notes drifted away. People lingered in the silence, some with heads bowed, and a number sinking to their knees.

Better check on Mother. Ellie turned and stumbled past the somber crowd. Many of the folks had dark circles under their eyes, most likely from tending their own sick. Fear covered the place like a cloud of ash.

With her own self, she wasn't sure how one foot moved in front of the other in this deep weariness that had settled over her. Only, somehow, they did. She marveled at the strong brown appendages, bare, since she'd not bothered to put on shoes in the last several days. They sent up puffs of dust as they moved–surely, ever forward–carrying the rest of her body with them.

Halfway to the wagons, someone touched her shoulder.

"Hello," Thaddeus said.

"Hello." Her feet stopped, and she stopped with them. "You did well with the service. I'm sure it brought comfort to those who lost family."

"We all need comfort now." Thaddeus rubbed his jaw. "How's Ivy?"

Ellie's shoulders sagged. "Neither better or worse. Jerusha says the fever takes a longer toll on the young ones. Ivy is strong and healthy. She said we should see a change in the next day or so, one way or the other."

Thaddeus bowed his head. "I'm sure the next few days will be long ones. We've had some difficult times on the trail, but this has been the worst." He studied the faded cover of the Bible in his hands. "The guides warned us, you know. Before we set off on this trip, we were told of the dangers. Sickness, starvation, loss of animals. No one thinks these things will happen to them. Until they do."

Ellie nodded dumbly, fighting to hold back the tears stinging the corners of her eyes.

Thaddeus glanced up, and his face softened. "Never mind all that. We'll pull through with the help of the Almighty. He holds our future and will guide us every step of the way."

###

Dan met Ellie beside the wagon, a smile plastered across his always-dirty face. "Oh, Ellie, Mother said to come and fetch you. But I don't have to, 'cause here you are!"

"What does she need? Is Ivy worse?" Ellie ran past her brother to the tent and pushed open the flap.

Ivy still lay in her normal place, but as Ellie bent down, she rolled her head toward her sister. The corners of her mouth pinched up a bit. "Oh Ellie, I feel better today!"

Ellie closed eyes and leaned back against canvas wall. "Ivy, I'm so glad." She reached out trembling fingers and touched her sister's hand. "We'll stay here a bit longer, so you have time to get your strength back."

"Yes, we will," said Mother from the corner where she was gathering soiled linens. "Jerusha said since no one has been newly stricken for the last five days, we probably won't see any more cases."

Ellie pressed her fingertips against her eyes and exhaled.

"We are quite lucky, I'd say," Mother continued.

"God healed Ivy," Ellie said quietly. "Not luck."

Mother darted her a glance, her face shadowed in the semi-darkness of the tent. "Perhaps that's true. Whatever the reason, I'm grateful."

"May I have some bread, Mother?" came Ivy's quiet voice from the pallet.

Mother's face relaxed into a smile, fresh wrinkles presenting themselves on her wind-battered skin. "Of course you may, my love. Made two loaves this morning. Plain old johnnycake."

As Ellie headed out to fetch the bread, she caught site of Mrs. Martin. The slight, tanned woman leaned against her wagon, tears streaming down her face.

"Oh, Mrs. Martin, is Felicity . . ."

A tremor travelled through the frail shoulders. "She's in Heaven now, poor darling." Mrs. Martin held out hands, palms upward and stared down at them. "She was talking this morning. Said she saw the angels all around her tent. Then she closed her eyes . . ." The woman covered her mouth with shaking fingers. "She's so still." She gave a shuddering sigh.

"We did our best, her father and I. She's with her baby brother now." She glanced up at Ellie. "Perhaps it's for the best."

Waves of misery crashed against elation. *Is it for the best?*

Mother emerged from the tent and dumped a basin of water into the dirt.

Ellie walked over and stared at the small streams, slipping their separate ways from the larger puddle. A month to journey through

Idaho, and at least a month through Oregon to the Willamette Valley. Resources, tempers, constitutions. All stretched so thin. *God spared Ivy.* Somehow they would make it through.

8
Fishing

Ellie started from her half-napping state, a lazy bee buzzing away as she jerked her head. "Dan, you've got one!"

Ripples flew over the surface of the once-quiet lake. The enormous salmon struggled and twisted through the water to free itself from Dan's tiny hook.

Thaddeus rose from where he'd been lounging beside Ellie. "Dan, let me grab your rod. That one's a fighter."

"Nope." Dan's eyes stayed riveted on the end of the bouncing cane pole. "I told Mother I'd land her a big one all by myself. Here he is. I don't want anyone's help."

"Better let him, Danny. That's a big fish to lose. It could feed most of our family." Even as she spoke, Ellie knew her words would fall on deaf ears. As one of the middle children, Dan was pretty much left to run wild and keep himself alive. Her mother rarely had time for correction.

"No! Ellie, I can do it!"

Thaddeus stepped back, his hands up. "Suit yourself." He grinned at Ellie. "I remember when I was that age and always wanted to do everything by myself. Ended up in a heap of trouble, usually. I learned a lot."

"Let's hope he can manage," Ellie said, rolling her eyes.

The wagon train had arrived at Fort Boise that morning, only a few days away from the Oregon border. The lake beside the fort was fairly jumping with Kokanee salmon.

Quite a few children and young adults had come to the lake with poles of their own. Soon a sizable crowd had gathered at the bank, pointing and shouting at Dan's fish. The boy's tiny hands clutched the cane pole, knuckles white. He stepped back and tugged. The fish a blur of red and silver, thrashed at the other end.

"Oooh, he's tiring!" shouted Dave, ever Dan's partner in crime. "You'll land him for sure, Dan!"

Finally, with a mighty heave, the boy slung the fish to the bank, where it narrowly missed Ivy. She jumped and yelped, dropping the flowers she'd picked along the shore.

The salmon flopped in the thick grass, its mouth opening and closing.

"It's a fifty pounder!" Dave shouted.

"Maybe not quite that big," said Ellie. "It's the biggest one we've caught on this trip though, sure."

Dan reached for the flopping creature, but every time his fingers almost brushed the slippery scales, it would flip out of reach.

"May I help now?" Thaddeus asked.

Dan grinned and nodded, and together they unhooked the enormous fish and sloshed him into the keeping pail.

Some of the men and boys came closer, slapping Dan on the back and admiring his catch.

Ellie's little brother was happier than she'd ever seen, even at Christmas back home. His eyes shone brighter with each new snippet of praise.

He's so rarely noticed. As long as the two middle boys had plenty to eat, they didn't fuss for much, and seemed happy in their wild ways. This trip had taken a toll on them as well, and she'd noticed a hunger in their eyes whenever they watched their mother coddle Heston. She made a silent promise that she'd give them more hugs and snuggles, even though they did stink to high Heaven most of the time. If Mother had scarce time for discipline, she had less ability to enforce regular washing.

The boys moved down the bank several yards, but Ellie stayed in place. The day had been warmer than most, and puffy clouds meandered across the periwinkle sky. The lake was surrounded by trees, and mountains stood solemnly in distance, as if to warn them not to take this leisurely moment for granted.

Thaddeus stretched out along the rocks. "Such a happy day. Much better than the last few weeks."

"Oh yes." Ellie dipped her bare feet in the chilly water. "I've been meaning to ask you something."

"Yes, Ellie?"

She opened her mouth, but the words were harder to form than she'd anticipated. The last several weeks they'd sent wispy dark tendrils of smoke through her thoughts. "It's about God."

"Yes?" said Thaddeus.

Ellie watched thin ripples form on the pond, trying to imagine what created them. "If we hadn't come, Felicity would still be alive."

A shadow passed over Thaddeus's face. "Timing is timing. It's one of the hardest things to understand as humans. We all have a day to be born and a day to die, written out for us when God created us." He spread out his hands. "But we have hope in Jesus. This world is such a fleeting place."

"I suppose that's true," said Ellie.

"Someday this trip will all be like a dream," Thaddeus murmured. "The time is such a short passage in our lives."

"We'll never forget the journey. At least, I won't." She gathered up her courage and shyly added, "I won't forget you, Thaddeus."

He sat up quickly, and his eyes glimmered. "I hope you won't have to."

What could he possibly mean by that?

An hour later they'd landed several fish, though none quite as large as the monster belonging to Dan. The sun sank into the horizon like a golden coin.

"We'd better head back to camp," said Thaddeus, swinging Heston over his shoulders, despite the smearing of mud on his shirt from the child's tiny feet.

Heston crowed and clutched at Thaddeus's hair. "Camp, camp camp!" he sang.

Thaddeus winced. "Try not to scalp me there, little one."

Ellie grabbed the bucket, which now held three fish, and they walked along the narrow path, tiny peepers jumping out of their way.

"Come on, Ivy," she called. "Would you like to lean on my shoulder?"

"I'm all right." Ivy still moved slowly, picking her way around larger stones instead of scrambling over them like she would have in the past. She'd asked to come, and this was progress. *Altogether, there are so many reasons to hope.*

Faint pink tinged the mountain line, brightening the gray sky behind it. Thaddeus pointed it out to Ellie as they gathered wood. "Looks like a secret door to paradise."

As they watched, golds and reds and purples blazed through the sky, colors only matched by the late summer flowers dotting the prairie.

Four days after leaving Fort Boise, the group found themselves in a bowl-shaped prairie, tucked neatly within the mountains. Though craggy rocks loomed in the distance and deep bluffs lined the furthest edges of the earth, flat, desolate land spread out for miles. When they found a body of water, such as the lake, they'd cling to it like a woman embracing her child, until at last they'd leave it, once more, for miles of nothingness.

This morning was the first time in weeks Thaddeus had been able to steal away to meet Ellie. She'd greeted him without surprise, as though she'd always expected him. He knew no apology was needed, for they walked the same path.

After the fever swept through the camp, a spare wagon and team had been left from an entire family's passing. A vote had been taken, and the settlers decided the Herschel family should take the wagon all the way to Oregon. Then they'd sell the schooner and oxen and send the money to the family's only known relative, a sister who lived in Missouri. With this matter, Thaddeus dealt with alternate twinges of relief and guilt, but it did him no good to ruminate over these thoughts.

So Mrs. Herschel had a place to ride once more. Mr. Herschel was mended, mostly, and was able to help with chores and walk with the oxen for short jaunts.

Though several families felt the sting of loss, the wagon train hit a stride of work and function. They were forced to surge ahead or perish, and after death reached out with such lucid fingers, everyone moved faster. Folks rarely petitioned Captain Marshall to take longer breaks, to camp a few more days by the water. All knew the urgency, and as one mind, they worked together towards the goal.

A large, flattened rock rose from the grassy hillside. Ellie climbed a few steps to the top and sank down, tucking her feet beneath her. "I want to help people. You play violin and preach God's word. Jerusha knows how to help the sick. What can I do?"

Thaddeus clasped his hands behind his head. "I can't believe you're in a frazzle about that. You're always helping your mother. And running errands in camp for people. You work so hard to be cheerful. That's not easy."

"I try." Ellie tilted her head up, her faded bonnet hanging by the strings down her back. The sunrise bathed her hair, and it glowed like a halo.

"I love you, Ellie."

The words slipped from Thaddeus's lips unbidden, as though they were spoken by another creature. Weren't they? For they'd come straight from his heart, which he'd often thought a separate being altogether.

Ellie turned toward him, and the radiance shining from her face was from more than the sunrise. "Oh, Thaddeus." She touched his hand with a trembling finger. "Oh . . ."

"I shouldn't have . . ." he stepped back. "I mean to say, I should have . . ."

"You did exactly right," Ellie said. "I was hoping that someday you'd tell me." She closed her eyes. "Oh Thaddeus, how I hoped."

A pinprick of relief burst a thick membrane of fear and doubt that had formed, over time, around Thaddeus's feelings for Ellie. Warmth rushed through him like the geyser at the hot springs.

"Then let's hold onto it for this instant. So we'll have it to remember always." He pulled her into his arms and held her close. Her heart beat against his chest, and she laid her head on his shoulder like it had always belonged there.

Doesn't it? Oh, Lord, make me worthy. Make me worthy of this beautiful woman.

She pulled away and stared up at him, wrinkling her adorable nose. "My love, what would your parents say? They'll never agree to such a match. Mother doesn't believe I'm strong enough to marry or bear children."

His soul sank into despair, like always when he considered these matters. "I don't know how she can say that. You're the strongest woman I know."

She curled her fingers around his hand. "I wonder. Sometimes I feel like part of her mind is stuck in the past. She can't see truth for what it is, only what it used to be."

Thaddeus touched her shoulder. "Ellie, I won't lead you to the foot of a mountain we can't climb. Marriage is impossible. For now. When we arrive in Oregon, circumstances are bound to change. Perhaps your mother will realize how strong you've become. When you reach your father's homestead, maybe he'll help her to understand."

"Perhaps." The sides of her mouth sank.

Thaddeus fought the urge to kiss her until she smiled again. "Even though it would be nice to have the blessings of our parents, we're both grown now, Ellie."

She folded her thin fingers around his own and lifted her chin. "Though I want nothing more than to serve the Lord by your side for always, wherever He leads, let's not bring anymore hardship to our folks on the trail. After we reach our homes and settle our families, we can discuss these matters once more."

"I agree." Thaddeus closed his eyes, willing his racing mind to calm, his overeager words to cease their errant tumbling. "We should be patient. From what we've seen of the maps, our towns are only three days' ride from each other."

"For now, we'll still meet to sing, won't we, dear Thaddeus?" Ellie asked.

He smiled down at her. "Of course. The rest must be left in God's hands."

9
Rapids and Wondering

Ellie repositioned the stout stick and struck the shiny, black surface of ice, mustering the strength of five months on the trail. She managed to etch a thin scratch, lined by tiny frozen shavings. Leaning back, she took a deep breath. Hopefully, this struggle wouldn't be an indication of the day. *Maybe a rock would break it.* A quick glance of the campsite brought no inspiration. *Perhaps Thaddeus has a hammer or mallet I can borrow. No, I won't bother him this early. I can figure this out on my own.*

True to his word, Thaddeus hadn't brought up the idea of marriage again. But he couldn't hide the tenderness shining from his face when he caught her eye from across the camp. The few times they'd met to sing the pledge had hung between them like a golden drop of honey suspended in the air. Neither of them had mentioned it. The hope was too precious, and too easily destroyed.

They'd crossed into Oregon a week ago. A ragged cheer had sprung up from the group at the first sight of Mount Hood, rising like a beacon over countless other mountain ranges. Unfortunately, over the next several days the mountain appeared to stay the same distance away, though their tired feet plodded mile after mile.

Ellie wondered when she had become numb to hope. It must have been one of these repetitive days that her brain had finally whispered 'enough.' They were never going to reach their home. They'd live out the rest of their days in this desolate land, until their feet gave out and they died on the trail, a group of wizened corpses.

God will bring us through. The thought swelled up in her spirit, and despite the cold, she was filled with warmth. Hitting the ice with new gusto, she finally broke through to a decent amount of water at the bottom of the pail. She dumped the contents into the cast iron kettle they used for almost everything and lugged it to the fireside.

Mother plucked a chicken, the last from the Boise Fort. The poor bird had ridden along for weeks, faithfully giving its one egg, until this morning, when Dan had found it frozen stiff, pitiful feet stuck up in the air. Ellie hoped the fowl truly died of the cold and not some dread disease they would all catch by eating it.

Ellie hung the pot over the fire and gave her mother a sideways glance. Ever since Ivy had come down with the fever, Mother had been acting a bit . . . strange. Sometimes she'd mutter to herself, or swat at flies no one could see.

Ellie had asked Jerusha about it, and the old woman had shrugged. "Trail madness. Some people get over it, soon as they've settled into their new place." Her eyes, deep in wrinkles, held sparks of sympathy. "And some always carry the trail with them."

Could anyone survive such a journey without a touch of crazy? The endless trudging days, the cruel gnawing of hunger in one's belly, no matter what tidbits they'd been able to scrounge. Nights of restless slumber on the rock-hard ground in sweltering heat or freezing cold. But thousands had gone before, and more would come after them.

Dan ran up to her, his trousers so tattered they were hardly decent, even for a boy of five. "Word's going 'round. We'll be reachin' an outpost in the next few hours."

"Glory be." Ellie dropped a handful of cornmeal into the boiling water, stirred, then dropped in another handful. "Maybe they'll have fresh milk."

"And sugar?" Dave's eyes shone with hope.

"Perhaps," said Ellie. "At any rate, they'll have different choices than fish and johnnycake." *And diseased chickens.*

Dan clapped his hands and danced around the fire. "Yay! Yay! Yay!"

Heston tottered out of the tent, rubbing his eyes with a tiny fist. "Yay!" he said, joining his brother by the fire.

"You're too close, darling. Let's scoot back." Ellie picked up Heston and moved him a safer distance away. She gave him a hunk of bread from yesterday to chew on.

"This chicken's ready," said Mother, staring down at the plucked bird. "Soon as you all eat that porridge, I'll start it boiling."

"Mother, we don't have time to cook a chicken. We'll be breaking camp in the next twenty minutes." Ellie held up a clean flour sack. "Why don't you put it here? I'll pop it into the water bucket. Plenty of ice to keep it cool for the next few hours. We'll have a feast at lunch time," she added with a twinge of doubt. *That bird was scrawny.*

"A feast!" Dan twirled wildly.

"Child, you're going to scorch your britches," Ellie warned. "Not that it'll make them much worse. I must attempt some mending before we reach civilization."

She glanced up. Her mother still held the chicken, her eyes glassy and empty.

"Mother," Ellie raised her voice. "Let's put the chicken here." She shoved the pail a bit closer.

"Lunch. Of course." Her mother tucked the chicken into the flour bag with fumbling fingers and rose from the rock she'd been sitting on. She lifted her hands, covered in feathers and muck, to her hair, which hung over her face in greasy, snake-like strands. "I'd best tidy myself, child."

"Here, Mother." Ellie placed the bag with the chicken into the pail and slung it into a rope holster on the side of the wagon. With a damp towel, she wiped her mother's hands and face clean. "Sit right down and I'll fix your hair. Ivy, get the boys to help you take down the tents, please."

Ivy, who had been watching the proceedings with wide eyes, nodded and rushed to the tent without a word.

Ellie pulled her own small comb from her apron pocket and jerked through the knots and tangles in her mother's hair one section at a time. When they'd started the Oregon journey, only a few bright streaks of silver had run through Mother's bright chestnut curls. Now her hair was close to completely gray.

"Don't know what your father's going to think of me," Mother muttered. "My figure's gone to skin and bones, and I've lost two teeth. I'm an old hag."

"Oh, Mother." Though Ellie tried to keep her tone bright, her heart plummeted. Mother had never quibbled about appearance, but she was, after all, a woman. Of course she would worry. "Father will love you more than ever he did. Aren't you bringing his children home? He's going to be thankful you're alive and returned to him."

Her mother looked up through tears. "I hope you're right."

Could love be unconditional? Was that the kind of love she could hope to have with Thaddeus?

Ellie smoothed her mother's hair as best she could and twisted it up in a neat knot at the nape of her neck. "Even though it's cold, the sun's still burning you. There are blisters on blisters. Let's find your bonnet, shall we?" She felt more like she was talking to Ivy than her mother.

Mother crossed her arms. "Used my last one to tie up that cut on the ox's leg."

"I guess we'll see if we can buy a new one at the fort."

###

The path to the outpost would have only taken an hour if not for the water crossing. Due to recent rains the mighty Snake river was swollen higher than normal, and it boiled against its banks in rebellious abandon. A quarter mile away, the opposite bank was shrouded by a swirling mist.

Ellie was thankful that this section of river had an actual ferry, though the cost of passage was a dear two dollars per wagon. A handful of river crossings had no such service, and the men were forced to create rafts, which sometimes took days if wood was scarce.

Though the oxen had crossed many waters on this journey, several still balked when led to the ferry. The ones that faltered were tied to the back and forced to swim along behind. Men tied wagon wheels lest they slide off into the river along with belongings and supplies.

Ellie helped Burt and Tad prepare the schooners as best they could. Fortunately, they'd started off with sturdy crafts, and the drivers had taken care to maintain them.

When the trunks and crates had all been locked tight and tied off, Ellie gathered the three little boys and they huddled together, amid clustered families, to ride across the water.

"Ellie, will we be in the wagon always?" asked Dave. An unusual question for the four-year-old child, who usually let his older brother do the talking.

"Of course we won't." Dan put his hands on his hips. "We'll get to the homestead when we're grown men. We'll be big and strong by then, to help Father with the crops."

Dave burst into tears, his wails causing heads to turn among the other riders. Between sobs he choked out, "I don't want to be in the wagon until I'm a grown man, Ellie!"

Ellie pulled her brother close and stroked his hair, filthy and caked with mud despite the scrubbing she'd given him last evening. "Don't worry, Davey. We'll be home with Father before you know it."

"After I'm a man?" Dave wiped his nose with the back of his hand.

"No, silly. When is your birthday? Do you remember?"

Dave shook his head.

"Your birthday is December 7th," said Ellie. "And that's before Christmas. You'll be five years old." She gently tugged on his small fingers until they were spread out from his palm. "This many years. We'll be home long before then." *Lord willing.*

Dave stared at his open hand. "But my birthday takes forever n' ever to come, Ellie."

"So does Christmas," Dan said gloomily.

Ellie glanced over the raft. Thaddeus and his family were gathered on the other side, near the wagons. Mrs. Herschel was as disheveled as her own mother, and Francie and Maggie leaned against each other, eyes closed. Sympathy dripped into Ellie's soul. She'd forgotten they suffered from sea sickness.

Thaddeus caught her eye and gave her a weary smile.

We must try to meet to sing tomorrow. She ached to be with him, to rest on his shoulder and feel his strength.

Moments later, the raft came to a shuddering halt. Folks moved apart, barking orders to each other.

"Looks like we've reached the other side!" Ellie said. "We'll be at the outpost in a tiny bit. Let's hope for a good dinner tonight."

###

Ellie reached for Dan's hands. "Let's wash the sticky away, shall we?"

Dan jerked back. "Mamma says we shouldn't waste food!" He licked the last remnants of jam from his fingers.

"Suit yourself." Ellie said. Reconditioning the boys for civilization was proving to be harder than she'd thought.

Around her, the children settled back, patting their stomachs. True to Ellie's hope, they'd had a good dinner of jam, oven-baked bread, and canned tomatoes.

Normally, Mother refused to pay 'good money' for food they could make themselves. However, today was a time for absolute celebration.

"Read the letter again, Mother, please!" Ivy begged.

Mother pulled the stained paper, which had passed from who knew how many bags and satchels, from her bosom where she had tucked it. "Very well."

"Dear Martha and Children," she began, her eyes shining with the old happiness.

I have sent letters to settlements along the trail in the hopes that one of them will reach you. Postage is dear so I've only sent a couple, and I am unsure of which route you will take due to the Shoshone. If I'd known the risk would be so great, I would never have allowed you to come. But if you didn't, I believe we would lose the homestead. I must pray with all that is in me that you are safe and will arrive, as we've planned, sometime in November.

The boys are well and growing into men rapidly. They are a great help to me.

I have suffered an injury but am better.

Your husband and father,

Tom Davis

Ellie's mother refolded the letter with a contented sigh, giving the paper a little pat as she tucked it back in her blouse.

"It's a wonderful letter," said Ivy dreamily.

"Father really is waiting for us," said Dan. "I'll be seeing Robbie and Johnny any day."

Ellie's throat tightened once more, the way it had the first time her mother read the letter. She was glad to hear from her father and brothers. However, the letter had been dated from three months before. What awaited them at the homestead? And what injury had her father alluded to?

Mother picked up Heston and rocked him, humming a tune.

I won't spoil her happiness. A part of Ellie doubted her mother would listen, anyway. She resolved to pray over these concerns on her own. *We'll find out the truth in due time.*

10
Away

Thaddeus lugged his last bucket of water from the watering hole. Sweat beaded on his forehead despite the cool mountain air, and he paused to wipe it away. He poured out a bit of the water to keep it from sloshing and began the long walk back to camp.

Beside him, Francie hauled her own, slightly smaller bucket. She groaned.

"Are you all right?" he asked.

"Yes, yes. Wondering how much more water I'll have to carry before we get to our home. I hope we find a place with a proper pump installed."

Thaddeus rolled his eyes. "I'm sure Father wouldn't have it any other way. Or Mother, for that matter."

"Imagine. Staying in the same place for more than a few days. With a real bed!" She gazed at the sky with dreamy eyes. "And a clean pillow. Sheets with no sign of bugs."

His sister's wistful smile struck his heart. "Yes, it will be nice to be settled. I won't miss sleeping on the hard ground." *What if I never see Ellie again?*

How many days had it been since he'd declared his love? The Oregon terrain, with its never-ending mountain passes and water crossings, had been more physically challenging than any task they'd yet encountered. His muscles constantly ached. The strongest men found it harder to rise each morning. They'd had scarce time for visiting with anyone outside their family circles.

The end of the trail seemed so far, yet a scant few weeks remained until he and Ellie would part ways. *Perhaps forever.* He set his jaw. *I will figure out a way to win her hand. No matter what my father says. We will be together, even if it takes years.* His shoulders sagged. He'd gone over the options in his mind a thousand times, and had yet to figure out a solution. God had called him to preach, not work in a bank. But he had no organization, no seminary, no committee to send him out. Those accomplishments took years to achieve, and most churches wouldn't consider hiring an unknown preacher with no one to vouch for him. He couldn't begin that journey without making sure his family was settled somewhere, especially with his father still recovering.

I hope she will wait for me.

Something rustled in the brush on the opposite bank.

Fear tickled the back of his throat, and he put the bucket down. His hand settled over the handle of the hunting knife he always kept at his belt and he backed toward the bank of the watering hole, which was a small pond surrounded by thick trees and cattails.

A man Thaddeus didn't recognize emerged from the thicket. His knees peeped through holes in his trousers, and a sleeve from his felt coat flapped against his side, the torn part stained a rusty brown. Perched on his shaggy head was a bowler hat, a type Thaddeus hadn't seen since he left Memphis.

The man drew closer. A deep foreboding filled Thaddeus's soul, but he shook it away. Ever since his father's incident with the looters, he'd had a suspicion of strangers. However, this man was clearly in dire straits. He didn't appear to have a weapon other than a knife, similar to the one Thaddeus owned, tucked in his waistband. Nothing he'd done warranted bad treatment, at least of yet.

Thaddeus raised a hand. "Hallo."

The stranger glanced up and waved in return. "Good day." He pushed through the brush until he reached the opposite bank a few yards away. "Glad to see another living soul here. Can I get some assistance here?"

Thaddeus nodded to Francie, who stood frozen like a startled deer, her fingers pressed against her lips. "Take your bucket up and find Father or James," he said in a low tone.

Francie bolted up the path, water splashing on the ground around her.

"Be right over," Thaddeus shouted to the man.

"You'll find a path to the left, I believe," the man said, pointing.

Thaddeus located the semi-cleared path and pushed his way through low-lying bracken. After several crashing steps, he'd reached the man, who held out a calloused hand. His fingernails were crusted with blood, and smaller splatters had stained his clothes

"Billings. Jeremiah Billings," the man drawled in an accent Thaddeus didn't recognize.

"Thaddeus Herschel." Thaddeus shook his hand, then instantly wished for water to clean his fingers.

Billings appeared to be thirty, maybe younger. He carried a worn leather satchel over his shoulder, knuckles white from his grip. Shrewd eyes gleamed from beneath the unusual hat, and a thin moustache, barely the width of a pencil, rested under an aristocratic nose.

The man gave a smile–more of a simper, really–and Thaddeus withdrew his hand.

"Pleased to make your acquaintance," said Mr. Billings. "Truthfully, it's wonderful to see any man at this moment. I'd almost be glad for a Shoshone brave." He gestured to the thicket. "I was abandoned here, you see. Wagon train left me with a crippled ox. I had to put him down, and I've been eating on him for two days until the meat rotted." He spread out his hands. "So no ox, no wagon, no mule."

Explains the blood stains. Thaddeus exhaled, and guilt began to replace his suspicion. "I'm sorry to hear that. Why'd they leave you out here?"

"Funny story, that." Mr. Billings scratched his scraggly beard. "Seems as though the wagon-master took a disliking to me. He weren't Christian, that man." He gave Thaddeus a slanted look.

"I see," Thaddeus said, trying not to show the flaming distrust licking at his mind.

Mr. Billings picked up another, larger rucksack. "I've already packed up my tent, hoping a wagon train might be along today. If you would kindly introduce me to your wagon captain, I'll work matters out with him. I'd like to join your train, at least until I get out of this God-forsaken country."

Thaddeus jerked his head toward camp. "Let's go. I'll find Captain Marshall." He led the way down the path, his mind buzzing. They'd left an outpost three days ago, and without a horse or mule it would have been foolhardy for Mr. Billings to try to walk back on his own. Still, he must've done something horrible to be left behind. He chided himself. *You don't know that. Maybe the wagon master was the evil one.* They'd had their own share of terrible leadership with Captain Reckon, the trail boss before Captain Marshall. Why, he'd aided and abetted a pair of kidnappers.

One thing was certain, however, and he wouldn't let it go for the sake of formality. "This land is not God-forsaken, Mr. Billings," he said over his shoulder. "Far from it."

"Ah." Mr. Billings doffed his hat. "Meant no disrespect."

Thaddeus remained silent for the rest of the walk.

Fireflies flickered in the dusky night, and lanterns glowed from wagons and tent poles. Folks worked in the last faint glimmers of twilight, before the true darkness settled in, snatching their productive moments until the next day.

Ellie tied the last thread of her quilt square and held it up. A crimson and green dragonfly fluttered around a cattail. The crimson was plain muslin dyed with currants. The green and brown snippets had been scavenged from clothes too far gone to mend.

"Oh, Ellie, how lovely!" exclaimed Francie, who was embroidering a pillow cover beside her. "How many squares have you finished?"

"This one is eight of nine," said Ellie, with satisfaction. "My first quilt."

Jerusha nodded from across the fire. "You'd better get a move on if you want to complete the last one. Only ten days until we reach Oregon City."

"Yes. Though there's a month's journey before we reach our homestead in Cottage Grove," replied Ellie.

"And my father's bank in Eugene," said Maggie, who crocheted a doily beside Francie. The dainty handcraft seemed ludicrous in the settings, but the girls treated the piecework like precious jewels.

"It's hard to believe we'll be arriving in such a short time." Francie folded her material and tucked her feet under her patched skirt. "I don't even allow myself to long for it anymore. I can't imagine what it will be like."

"Ladies, I believe our time's up." Jerusha stood and began to gather the supplies scattered over the log she'd been sitting on. "Don't want to burn too much wood, and I'm sure your mothers want you home to rest. No one likes crosspatches in the morning."

As Ellie packed her materials, Francie nudged her. "I noticed Mr. Billings ate with your family again tonight."

Ellie shrugged. "My mother feels sorry for him. The man was left with nothing and since we have vittles, we should share them. The other folks on the wagon train have also helped."

She tried to speak brightly. In truth, she didn't like Mr. Billings. Twice he had kissed her hand, and his lips felt cold and dead, like those of a corpse. When he'd supped with her family, he'd taken slow bites, watching her with lidded eyes from across the fire. The tale he'd spun had been a sad story. The poor travelling salesmen, searching for a new life and abandoned by evil men. She wondered how much of the dreary tale was true.

"Ellie, you'd better watch yourself," Francie interrupted her dark thoughts. "The whole wagon train sees how he looks at you. Mama says he's got his cap set."

"Francis Herschel!" Ellie snapped. "You shouldn't talk like that! We know nothing about him. Besides, my mother would never allow it." *I love your brother and your brother loves me.* She'd never share these feelings with Francie, who had no aptitude for discretion.

"Still." Francie folded her arms. "I'd be careful. Girls find their whole lives planned out for them with no idea how they got that way, especially girls like you, from a poor family with too many mouths to feed."

"I . . . ooh." Ellie's throat tightened, and she fought back tears.

Francie covered her mouth, and her eyes widened. "I'm sorry, Ellie, I went too far."

No longer able to speak, Ellie turned and stumbled back to the Davis wagons, hot anger burning white before her eyes. *Mother would never force me to marry a man against my will. Neither would Father.* This brought up the same unpleasant thought that haunted her waking moments. *Will they let me marry anyone? Will Thaddeus and I have to elope?*

The thought of her mother's heart, broken by betrayal, was almost more than she could bear. Could she hurt her so badly, even for the man she loved?

And Francie. Obviously, she only echoed her family's thoughts on poor people marrying outside of their status. When push came to shove, would Thaddeus go against his family's wishes and risk disownment?

###

Ellie paused to watch as the sun rose quickly over the mountains, like an egg yolk spreading over the surface of a pan. Her feet were damp from moving through the dew-soaked grass, and she pulled her cloak around her shoulders and tried not to worry. Thaddeus hadn't joined her for their morning song for over a week. His mother was poorly, or so Maggie had confided.

He can't be jealous of Mr. Billings.

As agreed on that day on the hillside, they hadn't discussed their feelings for one another again. What reason could he have to doubt her? *I must talk to him. Give him assurance.*

She gathered a handful of sparse wood and added it to her basket. Shielding her eyes, she peered down the slope where her brothers and sister filled their own containers.

She opened her mouth to call them back to the wagon.

"Ellie."

Thaddeus stood behind her, his violin in hand. His eyes were filled with sorrow and concern.

She wanted to fling herself into his arms, to pledge her love forever. She'd marry him today if he so desired. She held herself back from first impulse, instead creeping closer to him, within arms-length.

"Good morning, Thaddeus." Her heart pounded. Surely, he could hear it.

"Good morning." Thaddeus searched her face, an anxious gesture he'd never done before. "I have news."

"Oh?" asked Ellie.

"A group of folks have been talking. They don't want to risk going down Laurel Hill. My father is one of them."

"Then how will they . . . How will you?"

"My parents have decided to take a different road—one with a river crossing. If the river's down, it'll take less time." A muscle in his cheek twitched. "It's a gamble, but that's my father for you."

"When—when are you . . ." she dreaded the answer.

"We should reach the parting of ways today, perhaps by lunch."

"Oh . . . Thaddeus." Pain seared her chest, like an iron-hot arrow, shot straight through her heart. Any other words caught in her throat and refused to be spoken.

"Ellie . . ." the word was scarcely above a whisper. "You still feel for me, don't you?"

His face was boyish, his words pleading.

"With all my being, Thaddeus. Always." She glanced back down the slope. Ivy wove a crown of flowers and the boys were happily wrestling in the grass. "Still . . .I wonder. How will we be . . . us? How will this be possible?"

Thaddeus lifted his chin. "I will find you. Once all is settled with Mother and Father. I believe God has brought us together. Promise you'll give me time. Will you wait for me?"

"For all my life," Ellie murmured.

Thaddeus reached down and gave her a sweet, tender kiss, swift as a hummingbird's flight.

"Ellie?"

Ivy, Dan, Dave, and Heston huddled together, staring at them.

"Ahem. Children. Good morning." A pink stain crept into Thaddeus's cheeks. "Um. I bid you farewell." He picked up his violin, which had been set aside during the hasty embrace, and stumbled back down the hill.

The boys skipped in front of Ivy and Ellie.

"I know what Thaddeus did," Ivy whispered fiercely. "He kissed you!"

"Oh, Ivy, please don't tell anyone," pleaded Ellie. "The Herschel's are leaving the wagon train. He was saying goodbye. I may never see him again."

"I'm not a tell-a-tale." Ivy put her hands on her hips. "But you'd better not let any men kiss you ever again."

"Silly Ivy," said Ellie. Excitement and sadness filled her in equal amounts, and she didn't know how she'd face the inevitable goodbye in mere hours.

###

Ellie stepped back from Francie's surprisingly fierce hug.

"Write me, oh, please write me!" Francie babbled through her tears. "You're the best friend I ever had!"

Wails carried through the camp as other people bid farewell. Women who'd barely spoken throughout the journey's duration clung to one another like sisters.

Even the new immigrants, who had joined them in Nebraska, had been with the train for almost four months. They'd been like a small travelling town. A mood, somber as the days after the fever, hung over the crowd of travelers.

Ellie pulled her last pair of nice gloves from her apron and handed them to Francie. "May your journey be short and safe."

"Thank you." Francie rubbed the gloves against her cheek. "I'll wear them on the first day in our new home." She bounced on her toes. "I can't wait until we get there! And the best part is, Stan's family is coming with our group." She gave the unfortunate fellow a little wave. He paused, cheeks reddening, and turned the other way.

"How . . . nice for you," said Ellie.

Francie leaned forward. "I hope my brother doesn't stay in the dumps forever," she said in a conspiratorial tone. "He seems heartbroken."

"Really?" Ellie struggled to keep the emotion from her voice. "Why would you say that?"

Francie patted her gloves and slid them into her valise. "Oh, I'm fairly sure he's smitten with someone in this wagon train. Been wondering about it for a while now. Haven't been able to get him to spill a name." She tapped her chin. "Strange, since he usually tells me all his secrets."

"Indeed?" Ellie fought to keep her lips from twitching.

"Francie, we're leaving now," Maggie approached the two young women. "Ellie, good journey."

"Good journey." Ellie hugged the younger girl. "Our town is only a few days ride from your city. Maybe we will see each other again someday."

"Perhaps," said Francie. "God only knows." She squeezed Ellie's hand and went to join the group preparing to leave.

Mr. Billings was off to the edge of the crowd, but somehow, when Ellie glanced up, he had inched closer.

Ellie darted behind a wagon and peered out.

Mr. Billings removed his hat and scanned the crowd, his eyes narrowing. He tapped his chin and moved away.

Ellie left the shelter of the schooner. *I'd better see how Mother is faring. She's probably doing a secret celebration dance since Mrs. Herschel is leaving.*

Then she saw Thaddeus. He stood amid several men, smiling and shaking hands. He'd won the entire group over with his music and preaching. Ellie stared at him. So many things she hadn't noticed. The way he moved his hands when he talked, fluid and graceful, like when he played his violin. He listened intently when someone spoke to him, as though that person was the most important being on Earth.

I shouldn't stare. Someone is bound to notice, especially Francie. What if something happens and this is the last time I see him?

Catching her gaze, he moved toward her, as though their eyes were magnets and he couldn't pull himself away. He stopped a few paces in front of her.

"Miss Davis." He gave her a short, curt bow, but his eyes begged her to hold inside all the promises they'd spoken and the songs they'd sung together in the hills.

"I will," she said out loud, though the words would have been meaningless to anyone listening.

He leaned forward. "I will come for you," he mouthed, and tipped his hat. Wagon wheels rumbled, and he bent down to retrieve his fiddle.

She turned away so he wouldn't see the tears streaming down her cheeks.

Mr. Billings came up beside her. He folded his arms and smirked.

Ellie whirled away and stumbled back to her family's wagon. "That hateful, hateful man!" she whispered. *How dare he ruin such a precious moment!*

As the train pulled out, Thaddeus's final gift to her floated through the air. The sweet notes of her favorite hymn, one they'd written together.

> *"And I will come where you are,*
> *Together we will awaken the dawn."*

PART TWO

I I
Laurel Hill

Screeching wagon wheels echoed through the trees, along with the bellows of oxen and men's shouts. Heston buried his face on Ellie's shoulder, whimpering.

"It's all right, Heston." She stroked his sweat-soaked curls. "We're going down the hill now. I'm holding you tight, honey."

She'd used an apron to tie her brother against her body as a sort of sling. This left her hands free while she navigated the steep slant, holding to saplings and roots. She'd done this a few times before, but Laurel Hill was unlike any slope they'd encountered so far. The terrain was lined with fist-sized gray rocks, most with sharp edges, and the path twisted and turned, the end impossible to see from the summit.

Somewhere down the hill, Mother was helping to brace one of their wagons. Ivy had joined several other children to help with the livestock already at the bottom. Dave and Dan were close but expected to make it on their own.

As she slipped and slid, she scrabbled for saplings and roots to slow her down. Sharp thorns dug into her hand, and she jerked it back, sticky with blood. *Must have grabbed a thorn bush. No time to focus on trifles.* One misstep could leave her with a broken ankle, or send her pitching down the hill, along with any unfortunate soul who happened to be in her path.

From habit, she glanced back to see if Thaddeus was nearby. *No.* He was gone. If she wanted a chance to see him again, she'd have to survive this horrible journey.

No wonder the Herschels had decided to take their chances with the other trail. Many had come to destruction on Laurel Hill, as could be seen by the piles of debris along the sides, and from what she'd heard, at the foot.

The entire day had been spent preparing the wagons for the long slide down. Spare oxen, horses and mules were sent first, most of them balking and bucking their protests. Their driver, Bert, had a nasty bruise on his shin from an errant hoof.

Mrs. Martin plopped down next to her; cheeks smudged with mud. "What if we don't make it?" she whispered, perhaps to herself. "What if I fall and die? God didn't spare my poor Felicity. Why would He spare me?"

Ellie patted Heston with one hand and rested her other palm on Mrs. Martin's shoulder. "We're going to make it. We can't give in to fear, not this late in the game. Imagine it. We'll be in Oregon City in a few days."

"I hope." Mrs. Martin said in a dull voice. She closed her eyes. "I hope."

"We can't give up now," Jerusha said, settling beside Ellie.

"How did your wagon fare?" Ellie asked.

"Next to go," Jerusha said. "Some of the men climbed back up to help bring it down for me. They bless this old woman."

"I'm sure they are thankful for your doctoring," said Ellie.

Mrs. Martin opened her eyes. "I'm not certain I can make it the rest of the way."

Ellie craned her neck to check the hill. Several more people were above them, making the slow descent. After they reached the end, the second batch of wagons would follow.

"We have to get out of the way. We can't stay here."

"I can't" the woman shrieked, her eyes wide and wild. "I can't make it, I tell you! Leave me here!"

Heston stared at her, opened his mouth, and added his wail to her own.

"This won't do," Jerusha said firmly.

"No, it won't. Mrs. Martin, grab hold of the sling. You can come down with us." Though Ellie kept her voice bright, her gut twisted. They'd been warned not to go down tied together. *I can't leave her here. She will surely be crushed.* She glanced over at Jerusha, who nodded. "Yes, take it, for goodness' sake. Be quick!"

Mrs. Martin's eyelids fluttered open at the sharp words. "What? Hold what?"

"Here." Ellie gave her the fluttering end of her makeshift sling. "I'm going down now, and you're coming with me. Get up."

She edged out past the shelf, her feet immediately slipping in the loose rocks. She snatched at a sturdy sapling.

To her immense relief, Mrs. Martin mutely followed.

"There you are," said Jerusha. "I'll be right behind you, dear. We're going to make it fine."

After much slipping and sliding. Ellie's feet hit the level ground at the foot of the hill. Rich relief sloshed into her spirit, thick as buttermilk.

She held out a hand to Mrs. Martin, who grabbed it and landed beside her.

"Over here." Jerusha pointed to a shady hollow where several other women and children were resting.

Mrs. Martin sank down against a thick tree trunk. "Thank you–for helping me," she whispered.

"Of course," said Ellie. "You'd do the same for me."

Dan and Dave ran to them, whooping and yelling.

"That was a splendid hill, wasn't it, Ellie!" said Dan. He grinned, despite the fresh scratches that covered his cheeks.

"That's not the word I would use," said Ellie. "Come here, boys."

She untied Heston from his sling. The children leaned against her skirts. Their high spirits quickly dissipated, and they dozed in the late afternoon haze.

Jerusha slipped a small canteen from under her dress. She took a sip and handed it to Ellie. "Give some to the baby. Peppermint water."

Ellie drizzled some into Heston's open lips.

"More, Ellie!" said Heston.

"No," said Ellie. "We'll go to the stream after Mother finds us."

As though conjured up by her words, Mother appeared, followed by Ivy.

"Well, that was an unforgettable ride," Mother said, settling in the thick leaves. "Hope to goodness I never have to slide down another hill in all my born days."

"Ooh." Jerusha plucked a lovely flower sprig with several broad green leaves from the grass. "Rhododendron. Lovely flower, but poisonous for the beasts."

Mother groaned. "Another malady to watch for!"

Jerusha patted her shoulder. "Remember all the mountains we've crossed, and the dangerous creatures we've avoided. This hill is the last of the worst, or so Captain Marshall said. This may be the hardest trial we'll endure in our lifetime."

Mother stared at her, her iron-gray hair standing out from her head in tufts. "I've birthed seven children."

"And lived to tell about it," Jerusha said cheerfully. "See? This is a tea party in comparison."

"I never considered that," Mother folded her arms.

Mrs. Martin rose on shaky feet. "I'm going to find my husband. Thank you all again."

Mr. Billings came by, his shirt sticking to his back in a thick patch of sweat. "Mrs. Davis." He doffed his hat. "Wanted you to know I oversaw the handling of your lead wagon, since Bert had to rest after his injury."

"That's kind of you," Mother said wearily. "I braced the second one all by my lonesome."

Mr. Billings replaced his hat and winked at Ellie, who fought a childish inclination to stick out her tongue.

"And here comes mine." Jerusha rose as her green gypsy cart trundled by. "Glad to see she's survived another day."

More wagons arrived safely at the bottom of the hill, until finally, they were all accounted for. Miraculously, only minor injuries had been sustained.

Folks rested and ate a late lunch on the small plateau, and then started the process all over again on the much shorter and less dangerous incline below. By the time they'd finished, stars glowed in the evening sky. Wolves howled in the thick woods surrounding them, and folks built bonfires on the camp's edge. Weary men and boys would have to tend these infernos throughout the night to keep the shaggy beasts at bay.

By the fire, Ivy leaned her head on Ellie's shoulder. "I wish Thaddeus was here to play his violin," she said sleepily.

"So do I," replied Ellie. A sudden longing for him made her eyes smart with tears. She brushed them away. *I will see him again. He's out there. He'll come for me.*

The fire danced and sparked. Quietly, Ellie sang.

"Jesus, lover of my soul,
Let me to Thy bosom fly,
While the nearer waters roll,
While the tempest still is high:
Hide me, O my Savior, hide,
Till the storm of life is past;
Safe into the haven guide;
O receive my soul at last."

The wolves continued to howl. An icy wind blew through the treetops, but the fire's warmth felt good on her tired skin. Too weary to pitch a tent or even drag out blankets, she'd soon sleep like the dead.

Her lips curled into a smile. No reason to embrace fear. Life would bring what it would bring. And, hopefully, home was right over the horizon.

12
Abernathy Green

"Water's low."

Thaddeus stared at the swirling, churning water rapids. "I beg your pardon?"

James swept his arm towards a wooden marker, nailed to a tree trunk. "See? This river crossing's usually twice the distance. Ferryman told me. Most times the raft can't operate. That's why most folks opt for Laurel Hill. They get here and are forced to turn back. We got lucky. Rainy season's running late."

Thaddeus closed his eyes and allowed the burdens that had accumulated on his soul the last few days to slide off into the dust."

The ferry was smaller than the ones they'd seen on previous crossings, but it seemed sturdy and was certainly large enough for the ten wagons that had come.

Thaddeus and James bound the wagon wheels with thick leather straps while Francie and Maggie made sure what was left of the family's possessions where tied down tight.

Thaddeus's mother, as always, cowered in the schooner.

Mr. Herschel stared at the wagon in tight-lipped silence.

Realization flooded into Thaddeus. *No wonder Father chose to come this route. Mother never would have made it down that hill. Safer to brave the rapids than to deal with her fits.* His jaw tightened.

How would Ellie's family fare? He wished he could ride back to the wagon train and share the news of the lower river. They were already days away. *I will have to put them in God's hands, like always.*

Soon they'd prepared the schooners, and the ferry began its crossing. The craft bucked a bit at the beginning. Thankfully, toward the middle the water calmed. Barely a ripple disturbed the smooth surface.

Francie stood by Thaddeus's elbow. "Isn't it wonderful?" she said. "Not only is our journey shortened by ten days, but we didn't have to brave the chute at Laurel Hill."

"Yes. I'm thankful," Thaddeus murmured. His thoughts were fixed on Ellie and her family. Would they make it? Would their wagons and animals survive?

What about Mr. Billings? His fingers tightened. He rued the day he'd introduced that man to Captain Marshall. *The way he leers at Ellie . . .*

The ferry reached the western shore, and folks began the process of hitching up the oxen and dragging the wagons through the mud and back to the trail.

Mr. Herschel gave Thaddeus a light punch on the arm. "Let's get back to work, son. Don't know where your mind has been, but I need you here. We're almost home."

"Yes, Father," Thaddeus replied. *And please, God, let Ellie be waiting for me at the end.*

The cheer rose from the front of the train and spread like prairie fire to the very last wagon.

"Look, Ellie, houses!" Ivy exclaimed, her sunken cheeks the healthiest pink Ellie had seen in a long time.

The valley lay before them. Nestled within the rocks and trees was a real town, with large buildings and corn silos and factories with honest-to-goodness cigar-shaped chimneys belching smoke into the blue sky. Horses and carriages crawled along actual roads, not hewn-out wagon ruts.

"It's wonderful," said Ellie, trying to shake away a tiny fear gnawing at the back of her mind. Though the arrival to Oregon City was an accomplishment, the family still had almost two weeks to go before arriving at the homestead at Cottage Grove. These roads might be smoother, but the wagons would still go at a snail's pace.

Mother was anxious to find her husband and boys. She'd already told Ellie she wouldn't be waiting around to join other folks that might be going the same direction.

"Too much arguing." She'd jutted out her chin. "These people will scatter like ants when we get to Oregon City. Some of them have yet to stake a claim anywhere. Many folks have decided to winter here. Snow could come at any time. I know where I'm going, and that's that."

On one hand, Ellie shared her mother's impatience. But her mother had divulged more sobering news. Burt and Tad had only agreed to be their drivers until Oregon City. Mother had failed to convince them to leave civilization when they'd only now reached it.

Mother walked in front, beside the lead ox. Her hair was in more disarray now, matted in fist-sized clumps. The dress she wore was only clean because Ellie had snatched it while she was sleeping and washed it herself. *Can I even trust her to make wise decisions right now?*

She brushed the thoughts away like pesky flies. *We'll find someone. Somehow.* She couldn't allow herself to give in to despair.

The trip down the road to the city was longer than anticipated. Men's fingers twitched around their whips, and women held back small children who tried to run ahead to the city below.

No blazing day in the desert, nor day of walking through the pouring rain had seemed longer, but at last they arrived on the level road, passing cows and horses grazing in lush green fields.

The beasts of the train bellowed and nickered at their cousins, as though asking how they managed to live lives of such leisure.

A young boy ran up to Mother. "Captain Marshall says there's a wagon camp at the first left of t'road called Abernathy Green. The governor allows folks to stay in the meadow behind his house. We can settle there and then go into town for supplies."

"Sounds like a wonderful place. Thank you kindly, young Wyatt," said Mother. She ruffled Heston's hair as he walked beside her. "Did you hear that, my son? Fresh milk and eggs for dinner, perhaps!"

"Milk!" Heston exclaimed. The little boy picked up new words all the time. Ellie sometimes feared for the child, who was skinny as a scarecrow. However, when he got a gumption to bolt away, she had to run with all her might to catch him, so she figured she shouldn't worry too much.

The great white house rose up like a fortress within a grove of trees. Behind it was the field. Schooners dotted the area as far as the eye could see. Hundreds and hundreds, more than Ellie had seen at any other camp.

Ellie couldn't help but search for the Herschel's wagon. Barring a disaster, they would have been there and gone several days before. *Still, the tiniest chance.* She closed her eyes. *I can't even imagine it.* Hope strained her soul, threatening to break it to pieces.

Bert came to walk beside her. "We may have to spread out. Don't see where all the wagons in our train can fit."

"Does it really matter?" asked Ellie. "We aren't going to stay together anyway."

"I suppose that's true." He lowered his voice. "I hate to leave your family like this, Ellie, but Tad's insisting. He has an uncle living in these parts, and guaranteed jobs for both of us."

"I understand," Ellie managed to choke out.

"Maybe your ma will find another group to join by the morrow."

"I hope so," said Ellie. She gazed behind her, at the line of wagons separating, already fanning out to find their own empty patches of field. These people had travelled and danced and grieved together for what seemed like a lifetime. Already they were passing, being absorbed into new and different lives.

Bert and Tad conferred for a moment and led the oxen to a sunken area in the field with enough room for both the wagons.

"I believe this will do for you, ma'am," said Tad. His eyes danced and his fingers twitched.

"Thank you, boys, from the bottom of my heart," said Mother. "Let's have supper and then I'll pay your dues."

"We'll get the animals settled while you make vittles," said Bert.

Ellie helped her mother set up camp as they'd done so many times in the last months. "I thought Bert and Tad would stay another day or so," she said as they fluffed the blankets and spread them in the tent.

Mother pursed her lips. "I made a decision yesterday. I should have told you, since you're not a youngster anymore. You have a right to know the family doings." She glanced up, some of the old fire back in her eyes. "We're leaving tomorrow . . . by stagecoach."

"Stagecoach?" Ellie clutched a flattened, straw-stiff pillow. "What will we do with the wagons . . . and the oxen?"

"We'll sell any non-vital possession," said Mother firmly. "I don't care if we have to break the wagons down to kindling and butcher the oxen ourselves." She caught Ellie's eye and her face tightened, then relaxed. "Don't you worry none, it won't come to that. Someone'll be buying."

She slapped the tent flap open and stared outside. "Clothes and food can be stuffed in chests and strapped to the top of the coach. We're going to find your father, and I'm not taking the slow way. Tom will probably snatch me bald-headed when he realizes what I'm spending, but I don't care anymore. I've waited eighteen months to hear his voice and see the faces of my sons. I won't tarry any longer."

"Oh, Mother." Ellie clasped her hands. "I was wondering how on earth we would manage! You couldn't have made a better choice. I'm so happy!" She hugged her mother tight.

"Don't go choking me to death." Mother laughed and gently pushed her away. "We'll still have to find a stagecoach going that way, with room for all of us. Bert and Tad will take two pairs of oxen and a wagon for part of their payment, so we won't have to sell those. Luck has seen us through this far." She threw up her arms. "Who am I to worry about this final short leg of the trip?"

"Not luck, Mother," Ellie protested.

"First light of morning I'll run to town and enquire about a stage. You and the boys can ask around Abernathy Green to find a buyer for the other wagon." Mother smiled wistfully. "Isn't that a lovely name, Abernathy Green? It sounds like a fairy land."

"It does." Ellie yawned. "Let's get these children to bed."

13
Boardinghouse

No windows brightened the tiny room, which was illuminated only by a lantern. A flame jumped and leapt from its place on a small table. Moisture and heat thickened the air. Warm water seeped over Ellie's skin, stinging bites and scrapes she didn't know she had. Mere annoyances compared to the bliss of settling into the clean water.

Months of only washing with soft lye soap or a bucket of sand and a piece of burlap were soaked away in seconds. Store-boughten soap provided by the kindly boarding house woman perfumed the air.

Ellie had never seen a bathtub like this one–made of porcelain and big enough to submerge her entire self. The washtub back home had been fashioned from half a barrel, and her mother would fill it with warm water once a week. The girls had taken their baths first, and then it would be emptied and refilled for the boys.

"Heaven itself must smell like this," Ellie murmured. She closed her eyes and worked a bit of soap into a lather to wash her hair. Oh, the luxury of clean hair! She could hardly wait to feel the clean, dry strands fall around her face.

A knock came at the door. "Hurry, Ellie," Ivy begged. "I want a turn!"

Ellie rinsed the soap from her face and hair. With such a large family, she'd never had the luxury of a long bath all to herself. Surely, this once, she could have a bit more time. Though one bath wouldn't wash away six months' worth of grime and even a basin made of pure gold couldn't cleanse the toll the journey had taken on their hearts and souls.

After pouring one more delightful scoop of water over her skin, she climbed out of the tub and rubbed herself dry with a clean flour sack from the stack in a small cabinet nearby.

Cool air wafted over newly scrubbed skin, and she stood for a moment, exulting in the sensation. *Never again. I'll never allow myself to get that dirty in all my born days.*

Items hoarded at the bottom of a trunk; the only wearables she possessed not tattered to rags, waited for her beside the lantern. Underthings came first, creased from months of travel, but gloriously free of dust and grime. The dress was from last winter, a thick woolen frock in two pieces with a long row of buttons up the back.

She tugged it on and surveyed herself in the mirror doubtfully. She'd become so skinny on the trail that the dress ballooned out like a sail from her body. However, the hem rode up a few inches higher than would be considered decent back home. *Mothers, keep your sons from the streets unless you want them to get a view of my ankles!* Nothing could be done, of course. There was no time to alter the dress, and Mother certainly couldn't afford a new one. She bunched the extra material under her sash.

Opening the door, she shooed Ivy in. "Scrub yourself down," she said. "And use plenty of soap."

"Oh, I will!" Ivy skipped over to the tub. "Isn't it the most wonderful bath you've ever seen?"

Mother waited for Ellie in the small room they'd rented. Her brothers still slept, curled like puppies in blankets on the floor. She gave Ellie's dress a hard stare. "At least those winter stockings keep you decent," she whispered finally.

"That's what I thought," Ellie whispered back.

Mother was considerably more put together than normal, with her hair brushed, braided, and coiled in a bun. The return to civilization seemed to be helping her spirits to an extent. Light glinted in her eyes, and her words came together in more coherent phrases. She still wore 'trail clothes,' though she'd washed them the night before and hung them to dry.

"Mother, why . . ." Ellie started to ask. Then she stopped. Somewhere on the trail her mother must have sold her best clothes, perhaps for blankets or food.

The furniture that filled the room was sparse and roughly hewn, but the windowpane was made of real glass, the first Ellie had seen since Nebraska. Cheerful curtains made of yellow organdy adorned the sides. A porcelain wash basin and pitcher stood on a stand.

"The arrangements are settled," Mother whispered. "Stage leaves in two hours. We should wake up these little 'uns."

"They need a dunk in the tub," said Ellie. "Will make being crammed in that small coach more bearable."

Unlike the girls, the boys were taken to their baths with protests and screams.

After everyone was clean, all belongings were packed and the family gathered around the boarding house communal table.

Ellie took a nibble of biscuit and allowed the golden crumbs, dripping with butter, to melt on her tongue.

Mother clutched her biscuit in rapture. "Imagine, Ellie. Soon I'll have a real stove to make food like this again. No more hoe cake and fire pit porridge."

"And we'll walk right outside to gather firewood," Ellie added.

"Yes, your father said it took weeks and weeks to clear enough land for the house and barn." Mother held up her hands. "Can you imagine having so much wood it's a nuisance!"

Ellie swept the remaining crumbs from her cloth napkin and placed it on her plate. "Children, we must hurry. The coach leaves in ten minutes."

The children stuffed the last bites into their mouths. Dan picked up his plate and licked it clean, drips of molasses running down his chin.

"Danny!" Mother admonished him.

"Don't scold him, ma'am," said Mrs. Lantry, the boardinghouse owner. "These children look like they can use any scrap they get."

"That's true." Mother pulled Heston into her lap as he snatched at a fragile teacup. "We've had quite a journey. Thankfully, it should all be over soon."

Mrs. Lantry nodded. "You wouldn't believe some of the folks I've had here. Women with tiny babies near dead. Men scarcely able to walk due to frostbitten toes when winter hit too early." She folded her arms. "I'm glad you've decided to take the stage. Your wagon train arrived late. The snow could be here any day."

"We suffered many cold nights, but at least we escaped the frostbite." Ellie scrubbed the egg from Dave's face and took his hand. "Ready to go, little one?"

Dave nodded, a huge grin spreading across his face. "Will we go fast as lightning, Ellie?"

"Not quite," said Ellie. "However, I bet it'll beat those old wagons all hollow."

"Won't Father be surprised to see us?" asked Ivy.

"Mother wrote him a letter, but I bet we'll get there first," said Ellie. The tiny trickle of fear was back again. *What if Father isn't there? What if something happened to him and Robbie and Johnny had to go to an orphanage? Or they're keeping the homestead all on their own?* She shuddered.

Mother started to gather the plates from around the table.

Mrs. Lantry laid a gentle hand on her shoulder. "Don't fret yourself. That's my job. I'll call my Harvey and have him help you get your bags to the station. It's not far but you do have so many little uns to keep together."

"Thank you, Mrs. Lantry." Mother beamed. "We've had a wonderful stay here. I can't thank you enough for your kindness."

Mrs. Lantry said, "I came down that same trail, seventeen years ago. I decided I'd spend my time on earth helping others, fresh from the path. Soon the railroad will come, and the hardships won't be so numerous. Until then, I do what I can."

Mother handed her a few bright coins from her valise. "Thank you so much."

At the door, Ellie turned to Mrs. Lantry. "Have you seen a family by the name of Herschel?" she asked in a low voice. "They'd have two daughters, one my age. And a son . . . a bit older."

Mrs. Lantry gave her a wink. "Ah, the young lady has a sweetheart. Can't say I've met a family matching that description as of late. 'Course, I'm only one of a dozen boarding houses here, and we're all pretty filled this time of year. Can't keep my old brain remembering."

"Thank you anyway." Ellie hurried to catch up with the rest of her family, trying to ignore the sinking feeling in the pit of her stomach. *Thaddeus, where are you? Did you even make it this far?*

Mr. Lantry, a burly man who was shorter than Ellie and stouter than Mother, had been at the beginning of the trip, tossed their bags to the driver at the top of the coach.

"Save room for me," came a familiar voice from beside the coach.

Ellie turned to see a black bowler hat. Her knees buckled and she grabbed the side of the coach to steady herself.

"Mr. Billings, what on Earth?" Mother exclaimed.

Mr. Billings tipped his odious hat. "Good morning, ladies. What a pleasant surprise! I suppose we have chosen to take the same stagecoach for Cottage Grove?"

"I had no idea you were headed there," Mother murmured.

"Nor did I, until this morning," said Mr. Billings in his customary too-cheerful tone. "I found an advertisement for manual laborers in the area and thought I'd try my hand." He swept out his arm, almost hitting Dan in the eye.

Dan scowled and stepped back.

Ellie bit her lip. They couldn't very well take a different stage; Mother had been extremely–she hated to admit it–lucky to commission this one. However, the thought of several day's travel with Mr. Billings was too horrible for contemplation.

The man's smirk deepened, as though he noticed her discomfort and enjoyed it. He leaned closer, the foul smell of his greased hair insulting her nose. "I'm especially pleased to be in closer proximity to you, my dear."

Ellie glared at him and looked to Mother, but she was busy settling Dan and Dave on the top of the coach with the driver. Her mother had taken on a breathless, excited attitude. All movements were brisk and hurried.

"It'll be good to have you with us, Mr. Billings," said Mother. "I worried the boys might topple from the coach. I'll be thankful for another pair of watchful eyes."

"Of course, my lady." Mr. Billings perched in a seat among the trunks, placing his satchel, which was never far from his hand, beside him. "I will care for them like my own flesh and blood."

I just bet you will, Ellie thought darkly as she settled into the coach beside Mother.

The stagecoach driver cracked his whip, and they began the last stretch of their journey home.

14
Home at Last

A brisk wind caught the brim of Thaddeus's hat and sent it tumbling across the grass. He set down the axe he'd been wielding and chased after the errant object, catching it right before the fence line. Virginia, the family's one milk cow that had survived the trip from Missouri, lowed at him from across the wooden posts.

"Don't laugh at me, Ginny." He pushed his hat down a bit more firmly and retrieved his axe.

The Wilkerson family, a neighboring clan beginning their third Oregon winter, had warned that a large woodpile was essential with the long winter months approaching. Many a family, they'd said, had made it to the Willamette Valley, only to face hunger and cold when they arrived.

He gazed at the square, modest home his father had managed to purchase. The estate had recently been vacated by a family who'd moved to California. The respectable manor wasn't as big or as stately as their home in Missouri, but it was comfortable, with two dining rooms and a parlor.

Mr. Herschel had spent a fraction of their gold on the home. The rest was invested straight into the bank he'd come to manage. He'd already hinted the time had come for Thaddeus to take his position as clerk.

Thaddeus made excuses for the first week after they'd moved into the new house. His mother needed help to clean, unpack and settle in. The buildings and what animals remained must be prepared for winter; and Thaddeus was much more comfortable with these sorts of chores than his father. These tasks would only take him so far. Father would eventually hire men to take over these jobs. His request would become a demand, and unless Thaddeus wanted to be completely disowned from his family, he would be forced to comply.

"God, you know I hated working in the bank back home." His axe bit deep into the log, sending wood chips flying across the ground like furious wasps. "I mean no disrespect to my father." He gazed at the fluffy clouds, serenely drifting across the mid-afternoon sky. "You've called me to preach your word. I have no idea how I'm going to do that, but somehow I will."

Ellie. Her beautiful smile bloomed into his mind. Her family should have made it to Oregon City by now. *How could I have left her alone?* His shoulders sagged. The decision to part ways had proved a good one. After the river crossing, James had come down with a sickness and his father might not have managed without him. Agony had filled him throughout the trip. He'd left Ellie with that Mr. Billings, whom he didn't trust as far as he could smack him across the creek. *What if she's hurt. What if she died? We should have eloped before the wagon train parted ways. But Ellie's family needed her too.*

He set his jaw. This was not an occasion to lose faith. Many times in his life he'd had to put desperate matters into God's hands, and this was no exception. A week, perhaps two, and Ellie would be a few days ride away in Cottage Grove.

More than anything he wanted to thunder down the road, burst into their home, and proclaim his love for her. How could he face her father with no prospects to offer?

The pile of freshly hewn logs teetered, and he re-stacked them into a sturdier formation. Sap stuck to his fingers and the spicy scent filled the air.

Wiping his hand on his pocket kerchief, he sucked in a breath. Perhaps he could work as a clerk if it meant having Ellie waiting at home for him each night. He exhaled, white steam expanding into the air around him. Yes, he could do it. It wouldn't take long to save a goodly sum, perhaps apply for his own plot of land nearby. He'd always been handy at carpentry. A home would take time, but Ellie would be willing to wait, he was sure of it.

He imagined himself coming home with Ellie on his arm. *No.* How many times had Father warned he shouldn't marry 'below his station?'

"Besides, if I take the job, I will be in disobedience to you, Lord." He wiped the sweat from his brow. "And your will is far more important than my worldly desires."

Francie skipped over the path towards him. "Are you talking to Ginny?" Her hair was arranged in a carefully curled updo, and she'd wrapped a new crimson shawl, purchased from a shop downtown, around her shoulders. Her thin cheeks were filling out again.

"Nope," Thaddeus answered, without further explanation. *That's one of the reasons I love Ellie,* he realized suddenly. *She's one of the only people I've met who speaks of God in the same way.*

Sure, most folks attended services, prayed, and read their Bibles on Sunday. Few of them talked about God as though they knew Him. Like a father and a friend.

Francie plucked at his sleeve. "Where's your mind? Somewhere back in Idaho or Wyoming?"

"Sorry." Thaddeus grabbed the last log and added it to the pile. He hesitated and glanced at his sister. "You might as well know; I may be leaving soon."

Francie's hand flew to her mouth. "What do you mean? We've only just arrived!"

Thaddeus sighed. "We've discussed this. My life has a calling, Francie. It's hard to explain. I don't even fully understand it."

"How can you begin to think of leaving right now?" Francie twisted her hands in her shawl. "Father needs help at the bank. And Mother . . . She still refuses to lift a finger. Maggie and I've done all the cleaning and cooking. We had to chase rats out of the larder today." She put her hands on her hips. "Rats, Thaddeus."

"Mother will find a hired girl soon; Father will select someone else for the position at the bank. A man who will be blessed to have such a job." He put his hand on Francie's shoulder. "I promise I won't leave until we get a bit more settled. But I wanted to tell you. I care about you, Francie."

Francie bit her lip. "I still don't see why . . ."

"Please don't tell Mother and Mather for now," Thaddeus begged. "I'll explain things to them myself . . . when it's time."

"All right," said Francie, picking up an armful of logs from the pile. "Far be it from me to tell you what to do with your life." She rolled her eyes. "I find it hard to believe you'd want to dash off to some other adventure so soon after we arrived. Haven't you enjoyed having hot baths and fresh meat again? We can go to the store and buy whatever we want."

"God is asking me to take a narrow path," Thaddeus said. "I'm happy to go there. I've known for a long time now. The hardest thing is to trust Him to care for my family when I'm gone." He smiled. "I'm thankful for our time on the trail. It's helped me to see how strong you and Maggie truly are. If you made it through that journey, you'll do fine here, in Oregon."

Francie shivered. "It's getting chilly. Why don't you come inside? Supper's almost ready. Maggie and I made fried chicken and pickled green beans."

Thaddeus gave a low whistle. "Whoo, that does sound good. I'll clean up at the pump and be right in."

Compared to the bounce and clatter of a prairie schooner, the stagecoach ride barely rattled Ellie, though dust coated the interior and stuffing sprouted from the cushions like marsh grass. The seats were big enough for two people to sit comfortably, facing each other. Ivy squeezed in with Ellie on one side, and their mother fit on the other end, with Heston curled up beside her.

Ellie and Ivy grinned at each other from their cramped corners. Though they'd travelled in this unsavory transportation for almost three days, stopping only for 'calls of nature' and nightly stops at boarding houses, the speed was remarkable. Ellie could almost feel the permanence of home on the tips of her fingers when she stretched out her hands.

Mother's head jiggled against the side wall of the stage, her mouth open to allow for snores. New wrinkles that had formed on the trail were smoothed by slumber, her hair washed and arranged in a neat braid that formed a salt-and-pepper crown around her head.

Ellie exhaled. While happy to see her mother in such a state of repose, she still worried. Would all be well at the new homestead? What sort of home had her father managed to build? And the pressing situation. Were her brothers truly safe with the man who rode above them? Mr. Billings had been persistent with his attention on their nightly halts. He'd taken every opportunity to nudge her, brush up against her. He'd continued to kiss her hand when saying goodnight, though she'd tried to snatch it away.

She'd done her best to remain polite but cold.

That night, after the children were tucked in and asleep, Ellie tried to broach the subject with her mother.

"I don't like Mr. Billings. Have you noticed the way he treats me?"

Mother held the letter from Ellie's father by the lantern light, silently mouthing the words, though Ellie was sure she'd memorized it.

"Mother, did you hear what I said?"

Mother stared at her with glassy eyes. "Ellie, Mr. Billings might be a fearful flirt, but he's just gallant, that's all. He treats all the ladies like that."

"No, Mother, he doesn't. When we were with the wagon train . . ."

"I don't want to discuss it," Mother snapped.

Ellie stepped back , the words smarting as badly as a slap. "You don't want to talk about the way I'm being treated, Mother?"

"Don't speak of the wagon train." Her mother's jaw was set, her eyes glittery slits. "I never want to remember that time again."

"Mother . . ." Ellie stared at her. She had the same listless gaze of the trail, the same fumbling movements. *Will Mother ever be herself again?* She could only hold to the hope that her father would somehow hold the key to bringing her back.

Ellie went to bed glumly, her only comfort was that soon they'd be rid of Mr. Billings.

The next morning in the stagecoach, they were once again on their way, packed tight as ticks.

With Mr. Billings only a few feet above, she began to rethink her reassurances of the night before. *If he works somewhere in Cottage Grove, he's sure to find out where we live.*

She pillowed her head on her arm. *Worry won't get me anywhere now. Life would be perfect if Thaddeus waited for me at the end of the road.* With this thought, she fell into a restless slumber of her own.

Her dreams were filled with dark, indistinguishable shapes, with Jerusha's crow cawing in the distance. The screech of stagecoach brakes pulled her from the dream world, and she gasped awake. Gripping the stage's window frame, she peered out.

They'd arrived at a stagecoach office, exactly like the other ones they'd seen along the journey but . . . *This should be the one.* Her heart bounded against her ribs. "Wake up!" she shook Mother's arm. "Wake up, we're here!"

Mother bolted upright, her eyes wild and staring. "Here? Are you sure?" she clasped her hands. "Oh, glory be!"

Heston wailed from his corner and Ivy worked to sooth him. "We're okay, little one. We're finally here."

The stage driver opened the door and swept out his arm. "Ladies, welcome to Cottage Grove."

An unremarkable group of buildings huddled in clumps on one side of the street, casting long shadows on the road before them.

The structures resembled most of the ones they'd seen in other towns. A general store stood by a savings and loan on one side of the street. A boarding house, saloon, and dress shop lined up on the opposite side with a boardwalk connecting them all. At the end of the street a small post office faced a sheriff's office. But somehow, this place was different. *It's our home.*

"Hold up, boys!" Mr. Billings swung their suitcases and trunks down, then hopped from the roof of the stage, landing like a cat on the platform below. "All right now, Dan first." Dan jumped down into his arms. As usual, the child was covered in a fine coat of dust. He gave Ellie a broad grin. "Gosh, we had a fine time up there. I wish we could travel three more days!"

"Dan, what a ridiculous thing to say!" Mother scolded. "We're going to see your father and brothers today. Aren't you excited?"

"I'm cited," said Dave, as he followed his brother to land on the platform.

Mr. Billings swept Mother and Ellie a deep bow. "Here's where I bid you farewell." He fumbled in his pocket and retrieved a crumpled piece of paper. "I believe the mill I'm headed for is on the south end of town."

Mother gave him a broad smile. "I don't know how to thank you for helping with the boys. We'll ask you for supper one of these days, as soon as we get the house settled."

"I would be honored, ma'am." Mr. Billings gave Ellie a wink, then craned his neck to peer out over the platform. "I expect your husband will be here presently?"

Mother spread out her hands. "No way to tell him we're here. I'll inquire at the post office to find the whereabouts of the homestead, since I have the address on his letters. He said our land's only a mile from town." She bounced on her toes. "Isn't it wonderful, children? Our home is just a short walk from here. Our feet will take us there in no time."

Mr. Billing's mouth turned down at the corners below his moustache. "Surely that's not a safe journey? You don't know the dangers of this territory."

"We've made it through worse." Mother lifted her chin. "We'll be fine."

She marched up to the stage master who'd piled the family belongings on the platform. "Sir, is there a place we can leave our trunks and bags until my husband can come to collect them?" A softness rolled into her words, as it always did when she mentioned Ellie's father.

The coachman removed his hat and scratched his bald head. "Surely, ma'am. I'll let t'platform keeper know and he'll stash them away."

Mother pulled out her money pouch from around her neck and paid the coachman. "Thank you kindly for seeing us out here. The trip was wonderful."

Ellie's spirits soared. Here was the capable, sharp-witted woman she knew. Perhaps she could dare to hope she'd returned fully.

Mother motioned to the smaller carpet bags that held the family's most vital necessities. "Children, take as much as you can manage. Not too heavy, though, all right?"

Ellie chose the heaviest of the bags, and the younger children picked up bundles of their own. Even Heston found a small burlap sack, but Mother took it from him. "No dear, you just hold a hand."

Mr. Billings hadn't moved from the edge of the platform. His eyebrows drew down over his nose. He reached for the satchel she held. "Allow me, ma'am."

"Whatever do you mean?" Mother protested.

"I'd be a foolish lout to leave your family with no escort to your new home," he said, giving a flourish with his free hand. "Especially with dark coming on."

Ellie's stomach tightened so hard that she clutched at her midsection.

No. Mother. Tell him no, she silently pleaded.

Mother bowed her head. "You're right, of course. I would feel more at ease with you in our party. Thank you ever so much. Your kindness to my family will not be forgotten."

"Truth to be told, well, you remind me of my own mother, rest her soul," said Mr. Billings. But his eyes never left Ellie's face.

Ellie wanted to sink into the earth. Perhaps somehow, she'd find an underground tunnel or some other way to her father's homestead.

She squared her shoulders and began to traipse through the dusty street.

Shopkeepers squinted at them from porches. Women and children stopped on the boardwalk to turn and stare.

"I don't blame them," Ivy murmured to Ellie. "We must look a sight, even with baths and clean clothes."

Ellie nodded but kept silent. Though the townsfolk didn't appear to be on the wealthy side, the women all wore pretty hats with graceful feathers, and the young girls sported fresh, airy smocks in bright calicos. Not a patch was to be seen.

Mother pulled out one of the many letters from Father she kept in her valise and smoothed it out. "Let's see. Our farm is out by the mouth of Reem's Creek, up on the hill. I'll just duck in and ask for directions."

Mr. Billings set down the bag and gave Ellie a half-smile.

Ellie turned away. She hated when Mr. Billings stared at her like that. *Hurry, Mother.*

If only they could reach home. *But Mr. Billings is coming.* She kicked a rock into the street. How she hated that this beautiful moment would be spoiled by a man she despised.

Mother fairly danced out of the building. "As I thought, a short way down that road!" She pointed down the right-hand lane from town. Trees, ablaze with autumn finery, rose on either side.

"How much land does your husband hold in the claim?" Mr. Billings asked Mother as they walked along, the boys skipping ahead.

"Fifty acres." Mother shielded her eyes from the waning sun, which settled behind the trees in golden brilliance. "A laughing brook bubbles from the rocks over a hill down from the homestead." She hugged her carpet bag. "Yes, my Tom is a poet. He's written me pages of letters describing it, I can almost see the place in my mind."

"Sounds like a nice property." Mr. Billings squinted, and his eyes glittered beneath his hat.

The tightness came back to Ellie's chest. *This man is dangerous. Why can't Mother see it? She's drunk on happiness.* This had always been her mother's folly. She'd allow excitement to overtake any good sense she had and spin her into a whirlwind that often left the rest of the family dazed and battered. Ellie's father was like this as well. *Perhaps why they wed in the first place,* she mused. Then another thought struck her. *Are Thaddeus and I as foolhardy as them? Is the notion of us being together just as misguided?*

No. God brought my parents together, and God will keep them safe. He saw us all the way across the country to Oregon. Thaddeus and I have prayed until our knees ached about . . . us. If God means for us to be together, He will make a way. Otherwise, may He protect us from our own notions.

Dusk approached rapidly now, and night birds Ellie had never heard began to call from the trees and fence posts. A colder wind blew over the road, catching Ivy's unbound hair and blowing it around her face.

Finally, there it was. A crudely carved sign, hanging from a gatepost. "DAVIS."

The gate crossbeams stood alone, with thick brush and trees being the only boundary. The last bit of sunlight broke through to mark the lane, barely wide enough for a single wagon. The drive twisted and turned, with no sign of civilization at the other end.

They all stopped and stared.

The tiny whisper of dread in Ellie's mind screamed for all it was worth. Ellie closed her eyes, willing it to silence.

"Here we are!" said Mother, her voice quavering.

They continued to walk down a cleared drive, following deep wagon ruts. Ellie remembered her father and the boys had come all the way with their wagon, instead of taking a stagecoach. How had her brothers felt seeing this new land for the first time, wild and uncleared? Fresh stumps greeted them on the sides of the road. A few spots of the forest opened as natural clearings but most of the area was dense with aged trees, growing interrupted for thousands of years. She tried not to imagine what creatures could be watching them from the darkness.

Had her brothers helped clear the trail? Of course they had. She tried to picture Robert, who was now fourteen, and Johnny, twelve. As the oldest two, she and Robert were the closest. He was a quiet boy who loved to read and recite 'pieces' for school. Johnny was scrappy and strong, like Dan. She suspected he'd been the most help to her father in the manual labor aspect of the farm. They'd seemed so young when they left, a year and a half ago. It had nearly killed her mother to let them go.

Lights twinkled through the trees, and within moments, the house appeared before them.

Mother let out a long breath, the color draining from her face. "Oh. Oh dear."

They could, indeed, hear a laughing brook somewhere in the distance. Despite this, even in the waning light, the house had problems. From the ground up until halfway, the walls were constructed of logs and seemed sturdy enough. Somewhere in the middle, the logs had been replaced with mis-matched lumber. Handfuls of straw and mud protruded from gaps in the structure, like hay from a horse's mouth. Tiny specks of light, showing through the cracks and the two small windows, were the only indication of some sort of flame inside. The roof sagged to one side, like a tired mule. The porch was hardly big enough for one person to stand on, and it buckled in the center.

It's so small, Ellie thought. *How are we going to live there? How will we keep warm?*

She glanced at Ivy, who raised her eyebrows in return.

The crudely made door swung open, and a boy stepped out on the porch. He was tall and lanky, with light brown hair flowing down over his shoulders. When he caught sight of the group on the driveway, he stood still, as though in a trance. The bucket he'd been holding slipped from his fingers and clattered on the porch, spilling water down the steps. "Mother?" His lips formed the word, almost too quiet for Ellie to hear.

"Mother! Father, Mother's here!" The boy whooped and hopped over the porch steps, missing them entirely. He ran to Mother, his ragged shirt flapping around his body, and flung his arms around her. "Oh, Mother." Tears streamed down his dirty cheeks. "Oh, Mother. Is this a dream?"

"No, Robbie." Mother clutched her oldest son. "I'm really here."

As the other children crowded around her brother, Ellie glanced back to the porch. Her father came through the door. He was thin, almost a skeleton, and he came down the steps slowly, grimacing as though in pain. Another tall boy, who she realized must be Johnny, followed him and took his arm. "Here, Father, let me help you."

Mother stumbled forward to meet her husband as he reached the bottom of the stairs. Her eyes were bright in the lights from the windows, and her hands trembled as she embraced her husband. "Tom, Tom. Just look at you. Oh, I missed you so much. Now I'm here, and all will be well."

"Yes, of course it will be," Ellie's father said. His voice was hollow, distant. The usual warmth and cheerfulness Ellie remembered so well was gone. His eyes travelled over his children, and the wrinkles over his forehead relaxed just a bit. "Everyone's here." He pressed shaking fingers to his temples. "You all made it."

Ellie ran to his arms, and Ivy and Dan followed, skipping over the stones and reaching their arms out.

Joy filled Ellie's heart, tempered by concern. *Father's embrace is so weak. What happened to him?*

Dave and Heston hung back, eyes wide.

Don't they remember him? Ellie stepped back to give her siblings room. *Dave was barely three when he left.*

Ellie's father placed a hand on each of the boys' heads and smiled down at them. Then he glanced up. His gaze fixed on Mr. Billings, and he raised an eyebrow.

"Jeremiah Billings, sir." Mr. Billings held out his hand. "I travelled part of the trail with your family and just happened to be passing this way. I wanted to make sure they arrived here safely."

Mr. Davis hesitated, staring at Mr. Billings's outstretched hand. After what seemed like an awfully long time, he reached out and shook it. "I'm in your debt for bringing my family to me safely."

Ellie shivered. She'd almost rather owe a debt to Lucifer, himself than to Mr. Billings.

Mr. Davis swept out his arm to his children. "Let's get you all in the house. The chill is coming in."

The small party trooped up the stairs and through the door, Mr. Billings included.

The main room was a tight squeeze for the party of ten. Two stools and one chair were the only pieces of furniture, so the children gathered on the floor around the fire. Other than a few pots and pans hanging in what appeared to be the kitchen, the walls were bare of decoration.

The mud and straw used to patch the cracks in the wall gave the house an earthy scent, mixing with unwashed bodies and a meaty aroma from a pot of stew bubbling over the fire.

Father gestured to the pot. "We don't have enough for all to eat their fill. Everyone can have a bite." His shoulders sagged. "I'm sorry, Martha. I didn't believe you'd be coming for at least another week, considering your last letter."

"Well, I made a change in plans," Mother said brightly. "We came by stagecoach."

"Stagecoach?" Ellie's father's cheek tightened. "How could you afford that?"

Mother rooted through a bag, pulling out bundles to set on the table. "Coach driver let the children go for half-price. Would've been nearly the same, buying provisions for two weeks on the road."

"What about your special knickknacks?" asked Ellie's father. "You had to leave so much behind."

"No trinket is more special to me than you and the children, Tom." Mother tugged open the twine twisted around one of the cloths. "I figured we'd need extra, so I bought cheese and bread from the boarding-house. All is well. Ivy, check that flour bag over there. I have bowls and spoons."

"We do have a stove on order." Ellie's father rubbed his beard, which fell to his belt like a silvery waterfall. "Might be in town by now. We'll check tomorrow. I wanted to have it here before you arrived."

"No matter," said Mother. "We've cooked in the out-of-doors for ages now."

Dan poked Johnny. "Hey, where do you sleep?"

Johnny pointed to the ceiling. "In the loft. We have straw ticks up there. Enough for all us boys, but we haven't freshened 'em out in a while."

Robert stretched his long legs. "We'd better fix up the room upstairs." His eyes settled on Ellie, and he gave a warm smile. "You should see your face right now! Father built a room for you girls down here. You won't have to sleep in the loft."

Mr. Billings rose from his spot by the fire. "I suppose it's time to see myself off."

"Nonsense!" Mother cried from the small table in the corner, where she was setting out the supper things. "You will stay here tonight."

"Of course," said Mr. Davis. "Not much room in the house, but if you have a blanket or two . . ."

I can curl up here by the fire," said Mr. Billings. "Beats sleeping in the cold outdoors by a mile."

Unseen drums pounded in Ellie's ears and her arms felt like lead as she helped her mother unpack. *Mr. Billings is staying here. In our home.*

She came upon her mother's second-best kitchen knife, wrapped in cloth. After checking for prying eyes, she hid it in her apron pocket. Unfounded as the fear might be, she'd sleep better with it under her pillow.

15
Snake

Candles flickered from silver perches in the middle of the table, glinting off burnished serving trays and bowls. Thaddeus scooped a dollop of mashed potatoes onto his plate and followed it with a spoonful of steaming gravy.

The house featured a formal dining area and table, but not, to his mother's chagrin, a breakfast nook. Therefore, she refused to partake of the morning meal with the family, insisting the girls bring up a tray to her room instead. She'd opted to dine alone for supper this evening as well, and her empty chair stood in defiance at the end of the table.

Thaddeus's father ate a bite of pork chop, and then wiped his lips with a fine linen napkin, one of the few that had made it all the way from Missouri. "A fine meal, girls," he said to Francie and Maggie. "You two are becoming quite the cooks. However, I've enquired in town for a maid to assist with household duties. Proper young ladies shouldn't have to ruin their hands with rudimentary chores, and certainly mustn't mar them with burns from the cooking stove."

Thaddeus glanced over at Francie, who stared down at her palms. His father's statement was ludicrous, as only a month before Francie hauled water and drove an oxen team with the strongest of men. Months, perhaps years, would pass before her palms returned to the soft, white state society ruled they should be. Francie enjoyed housekeeping, she'd told him so many times, and Maggie also liked certain elements of it. *Why can't Father let us be instead of trying to rule our lives? Our house could be a place of peace.*

Thaddeus worried for his mother. Though she'd always been prone to theatrics when displeased, she'd never withdrawn to this extent. He certainly hadn't expected her to carry on for a month after they'd arrived.

When he'd ventured into her room to speak with her, she wailed about how Oregon wasn't 'what she expected' and that the society was 'backwards and common.' Though how she knew he couldn't fathom, for she hadn't even visited town.

Yesterday, she'd suggested that Mr. Herschel send a search party a month's journey back down the trail for the possessions she'd left behind. How his father had guffawed at that!

Thaddeus picked at his last green bean. His mother was sadly addled. Part of him felt sorry for her. She'd been given little say when his father had announced the journey to Oregon. Through his life she'd never been content, even in their luxurious Memphis home. She'd always demanded more and better. As much as he cared for his mother, he was powerless to make her happy. Her contentment must be chosen for herself.

Maggie nibbled one tiny bite at a time. Since the death of her friend, Felicity, she'd stayed quiet and withdrawn, a shadow of her normally bubbly self. Usually she'd talk through an entire meal if her father didn't shush her, but lately she rarely uttered a word.

This journey has taken such a toll on our family. Will the money be worth it?

Of course, if he hadn't gone on the trip, he wouldn't have met Ellie.

Ellie.

"Excuse me." He rose from his chair. Taking his plate into the kitchen, he rinsed it in the wooden washbasin.

His violin gleamed on the mantel by the door. He took it lovingly in his hands and went outside.

A slight wind scattered leaves across the yard, and he was glad he'd worn his new muffler, made of beaver fur and purchased in the shops by his sisters.

He walked down the hill to the pasture. Zephyrs blew the hay in swirling patterns, rippling across the fields. Someday, a hired man would cut it. Until then, unseen mice and other creatures would scamper through its curtains.

Settling his violin under his chin, he drew the bow across the strings. Never would he tire of that feeling, the first vibrations and tiny notes that meant loveliness to come.

He played one of the first pieces he had learned on his violin at ten years old.

Sun of my soul, Thou Savior dear,
It is not night if Thou be near;
O, may no earth-born cloud arise,
To hide Thee from Thy servant's eyes

The last notes echoed through the hills and settled somewhere into the forest, perhaps into the hearts of grazing deer or slumbering sparrows.

A deep contentment arose in his soul. He was no longer forced to keep watch over livestock late into the night, or scramble over rocks and hills with a sloshing barrel of water. The twinkling lights of home were at his back, and he only needed to turn around and follow them to warmth and comfort. Of course, the wildest part of him missed the adventure, a tiny bit.

Boots crunched the grass behind him. "Hello, son."

"Hello," Thaddeus replied, bracing himself. The last few conversations he'd had with Father had been stilted and awkward. "How are you feeling after your day of work yesterday?"

"I'm fine." Mr. Herschel smoothed the front of his silken, store-bought waistcoat. "This bank is a goodly place. They are grateful to have me as the manager, and our money to store in the account. Plenty of eager investors coming in, fresh off the trail. Travelling season is slowing down, but people are getting settled in. Loan applications are flying in thick and fast."

Thaddeus polished the neck of his violin with the corner of his jacket. "Whelp, that sounds good."

"It is." Mr. Herschel frowned. "I see you're still playing that instrument. I hoped you'd have abandoned it after we arrived. Always told your mother we never should have paid for such useless lessons." The furrows on his forehead deepened. "We've winterized this place. You've cleared a mountain of firewood. It's time for you to take your place in the business. I've scheduled a suit fitting for you with the tailor in town. As soon as your outfit is complete, you will join me at the bank. You've put it off long enough."

Thaddeus swallowed and closed his eyes. An evening breeze caressed his skin with feathery fingers. A picture floated into his memory. On the way through a small town a few days before they'd reached Roseburg, an abandoned building they'd passed on the street had caught his eye. One wouldn't even know it was a church except for the wooden cross nailed to the side. The town hadn't been much in the first place, not even boasting a post office, but the few people they'd seen had greeted them warmly. A woman in the lane offered slices of bread, fresh from the oven, to the family.

That church. He shook his head. Why did it enter his thoughts now? There had to be a reason for abandonment–probably not enough people of faith to fill the place. Perhaps they congregated in another town with a larger group.

"Thaddeus." His father's voice broke into his thoughts. "The tailor said we could come first thing. We'll leave for town at dawn." His father's eyes were shrewd, appraising. "If the barber isn't available, Francie can cut your hair. And that beard. A bit scruffy, eh? You can see to that tonight."

Thaddeus took a deep breath, and then exhaled. *I must let go. I will never please Father, and I shouldn't try. I've chosen to follow God, and His ways are higher.* Peace flooded into his spirit. *Father doesn't truly need me. Another young man will come along who will do a much better job than I. I must follow what God wants me to do.*

He cleared his throat. "Father, I care for our family, and I appreciate how hard you've worked for all of us. God has set a different path before me, and I've tried to tell you many times. It's time I followed it." His words flowed out, strong and firm. "I will not be joining you at the bank tomorrow. I plan to leave the homestead at dawn."

His father stood unflinching for several seconds, varying shades of red playing over his face.

"Y-you ungrateful boy," he finally sputtered. "How can you turn your back on me like this?"

"I am grateful." Thaddeus bowed his head. "But I am not a boy, Father. God has placed a calling on my life I cannot ignore."

He moved past his father toward the house, violin in hand.

"Your mother has done this!" his father roared after him, his bellowed words echoing through the meadow. "Your mother is the only one to blame!"

Francie met him at the door. Her fingers crept to her lips. "Oh, Thaddeus. You've spoken to Father."

"Yes." He struggled for words, knowing the pain they would cause. "I'm leaving at daybreak."

She brightened. "You've decided to start at the bank after all?"

"No." Thaddeus placed his hand on her shoulder. He remembered the days when she'd been a tiny child. She'd chase after him and his friends, wanting to play the same rough games they did. She'd climbed the highest trees and won all the foot races. Their mother hadn't bothered to reign her in until the ladies of the neighborhood squawked loud enough. Francie had withdrawn into embroidery and china painting. Until the trail had pulled that toughness of spirit back out.

"Francie, I'll be going a different way. Like we discussed before."

"I see." A tear slid down her cheek and she wiped it away. "You'll come back and visit us, won't you?"

"Of course." He hugged her, despite her carefully arranged attire and hair. "If I end up where I think I will, I won't be far. I'll come check on you, and my prayers will be with you every day."

###

Streams of milk hit the sides of the wooden bucket in a satisfying hiss. Ellie squeezed out the last bit of white liquid and rose from her stool, patting the cow's broad brown side.

Fresh straw crunched under her feet as she moved. Rays of sunshine filtered in through slats in the wood, catching strands of spider web silk in a corner of the barn. The mixed aroma of cow, hay and sunshine was not unpleasant.

When they'd arrived two weeks ago, they'd found the barn a dung heap. Her father hadn't been keeping the two cows he'd brought from Oregon inside the barn because of the mess. Flies, maggots, and rats had overrun the place. Her brothers spent their waking moments keeping the woodbin full and hunting for game. Robert ran his father's trap lines, selling the sparse skins for pennies. For months, her brothers had carried the load while their father's wound mended, and hardship showed on their pinched, gaunt faces.

When her father and the older boys had arrived on the homestead, they'd built the barn first, adding in a small stove and loft. They'd lived in the barn for many months while they cleared the land and built the haphazard farmhouse.

Ellie eyed Mr. Billing's small leather satchel, hanging from a peg. She and her brothers had spent an entire day mucking out the barn so Mr. Billings could sleep there, after he'd offered to stay a few more weeks. Her mother had said he could continue sleeping in the house. To Ellie's supreme relief, he'd decided to stay in the barn.

She yanked cheesecloth over the bucket to strain the milk, and then covered the second bucket with a flour sack. They'd have fresh butter and buttermilk for the first time in months. This cow had lost her half-grown calf a month before. Wolves had cornered it in the pasture, poor thing. Despite this tragedy, the milk was nice to have. She tipped her head. Her mother might even try to make cheese later in the week.

Mother was a whirling dervish of action since they'd arrived home. She'd cleaned the filthy house, washing blankets and clothing. Any surface that could be washed was scrubbed twice a day. Already, Mr. Davis seemed stronger with his wife's devoted care.

She'd send Dan and Dave out to fish in the pond in the back of the property and the older boys to repair the house where wind whistled through the cracks.

School was something they'd have to put off until after Christmas. The drive to town was almost an hour and they couldn't spare the older boys just yet.

Mr. Billings spent most of his time chopping wood and running the trap lines, though he'd admitted he wasn't much of a hunter and brought home few pelts for his efforts.

Despite the house being cleaner and the comfort of being in one place, Ellie's mind was far from settled. Mr. Billings barely spoke to her. His eyes would rest on her in the same lecherous gaze, like a little boy craving candy. She avoided him, but in the tiny house, especially at mealtimes, they all rubbed elbows. As days grew colder, outdoor chores were done swiftly so bodies could rush back in to huddle by the fire.

Perhaps she was simply an untrusting, ungrateful girl, but she wanted the man gone. *And Thaddeus . . .*

She slammed the barn's door with such force that a board slid down from the side, dangling by one nail. Thaddeus would never come. She needed to get that notion out of her head. He'd probably decided to work for his father. Hadn't she seen the desperation on his face when he mentioned it? He would find another woman, a better one. One that was strong and could bear him children and care for his home. She must search deep into herself and find contentment here, with her family.

Will that woman sing with him at dawn?

She churned the butter with swift, angry movements, channeling her irritation into her work. After a few moments, she lifted the churn's lid. Milk crystals twinkled back in frustrating splendor, caught in the glory of the morning sun. *Too cold to churn outside.* Mr. Billings was in the house eating breakfast. *When will that man leave?* She thumped the top of the churn and hauled it up to the house. Perhaps she could sneak it into her room without anyone noticing. But her room wasn't warm enough.

The back room she shared with Ivy wasn't more than a closet, dark and cold as a winter root cellar. A stove or fireplace would catch the entire room on fire. She and Ivy had woken with the top layer of quilts slightly frozen this morning.

Ivy had begun to cry. "What if they freeze so hard we can't get them off?"

"Don't worry, we'll figure something out." Ellie had soothed her then, but privately, she wondered.

She slipped through the door with the heavy churn. To her relief, Mr. Billings was on the far side of the room, engrossed in a newspaper from town.

Her father was huddled in the one chair, wrapped in a blanket. It always took him a while to get up and moving on cold mornings. He was a shadow of the strong, hearty man he'd been when he'd left them in Missouri. He'd stepped in one of his own traps, in a moment of distracted thought. The resulting infection had almost cost him his life and foot, though he assured them he was now on the mend.

Mother bustled around the new stove. A pan of bacon sizzled on the top, and the aroma of fresh biscuits filled the tiny house. Though her usual limitless energy had returned, her eyes were too bright, her movements jerky and sudden. She'd often stare at a child, blinking, until they reminded her of an unfinished sentence.

Ellie set to work on the butter, and with the cream thawed, finished it quickly. She brought it to the small table and scooped it out with a paddle into a bowl.

"Oh, look at that butter!" Dan scooted over to the table and tried to snag some on the end of his rather dirty little finger.

"Dan, you scat!" Mother swatted his hand away. "There will be plenty for your biscuits when they come out of the oven."

"I'm all hollow, Mama," said Dan mournfully. "I might die before breakfast, and then you'll be sad."

"I didn't bring you all the way from Missouri to have you die of starvation here, Daniel Davis," said Ellie. "Go sit by the fire and wait like the other children."

Mother swiveled and put a hand on her hip. "Ellie, after breakfast I'd like for you to walk down to the neighbors. Mrs. Founder said she'd have some pumpkins for us, and I'd love to make some pies today."

"Pies, Mother?" Ellie's mouth watered at the thought of such luxury.

"Well, yes, considering tomorrow is Thanksgiving. We won't have a turkey. From what I understand, they don't have them running wild here like Missouri. I want something special to celebrate, and I think pie might be the ticket."

"Pie does sound wonderful," said Ellie.

She scrubbed down the churn and put it back in its place on the porch.

As she walked by Mr. Billings, he rose with a smile. "Ah, the beautiful Miss Davis. I heard your mother's talk about pumpkins. I'd like to contribute something, if I may." He pulled a quarter from his pocket and handed it to her. "That should cover it." His grip tightened on her arm, and he pulled her closer. "Don't tell anyone," he said in a stage whisper.

"Thank you." Ellie couldn't keep her nose from wrinkling. She pulled away from Mr. Billings and threw on her shawl.

She glanced back at her father. He was staring at her, a tiny glint in his eyes. *Concern?*

Maybe Father will make him leave now.

Slamming the door behind her, she stomped down the porch steps and out to the driveway.

She resolved to talk to her father as soon as she could get him alone. Which would be difficult. He mostly stayed by the fire, and there was always another member of the family there. And what would he do? In the past, she'd been his favorite, and he'd always protected her. In his present state he seemed thankful to rest and allow Mother to take the reins. In turn, Mother seemed to appreciate Mr. Billing's extra pair of hands so much that she didn't question his motives.

"You're not fooling me," Ellie muttered under her breath. "Wanting to help, are you? Well, I've never met a helpful snake."

16

The Founders

Trees rustled overhead, speaking in hushed voices of lost leaves, cold roots, and winter birds that fluttered from branch to branch.

Ellie stretched her fingers to bits of sunlight, soaking in the delicious warmth. No telling how long the light would peep through the dismal gray clouds; she savored each drop.

Thick clay lined the Davis driveway, molded into deep wagon ruts. The top parts were hard as rocks, but the deeper holes were muddy and filled with water from the previous days' rain. Ellie avoided this mud with care. Once stepped in, the foul-smelling substance would be nearly impossible to remove from her shoes. This clay was the bane of her mother's soul, and she kept a special pail by the door for the children to clean off their shoes or bare feet before they came inside.

In all the preparations for winter and housekeeping, Ellie hadn't been able to visit the neighbors.

Mrs. Founder, a widow, lived with four unmarried adult daughters, and a grandmother thrown in for good measure. Ellie's mother met them once, in town. *Apparently she'd chatted with them long enough to find out their farm had a good supply of pumpkins.*

Robert said the women had helped the boys through several tough spots during their first winter on the homestead, as they'd sheltered in the barn.

"Watch the grandmother, though," he'd warned. "She's a crazy old bat, that one is."

Ellie veered on to the main road, walked a few hundred yards, then untied the gate to the Founders' driveway.

A big yellow dog leaped from the woods to greet her, tongue lolling out of his mouth and tail wagging furiously.

Robert had described this animal, and promised he was friendly. True to his word, the dog licked her hand and whined.

"I'll pet you in a minute," she said as she tied the gate behind her.

Fields stretched out on either side of the driveway, and smart board fences ran along the way, with no gaps or rotten places. Horses munched the sparse grass left from the first winter frosts, barely raising their heads as she walked past. The dog bounded around her, stopping after a few steps to shove his head under her hand.

She followed the smooth path for quite some time, passing immaculately clean sheds, barns, and stables. The fields were turned over and resting in preparation for the spring. Hard to fathom the hours and days of hard labor it would take for such work. This was the life her father had brought them to, the fate of her brothers until they became men and purchased fields of their own. Why would he choose such a life? Her father's store had been a friendly place, cozy and clean. Each person in town stopped by at least weekly, and her father would lean against the counter and swap stories. He'd seemed content enough. Somehow, he'd been lured away by the promise of free land and a farmer's life. *I wonder if he's happy now.*

The large, square house appeared, huddled under a grove of trees. Behind it were fields of fruit trees, spread out down the hillside. Smaller saplings sprouted in the front, and beyond that, the trunks grew thicker and fuller, telling of years of planting and growth.

Something creaked on the wrap-around porch, and the sound became louder as Ellie approached. An ancient woman rocked in a chair. In her lap was what Ellie thought might be a gray blanket, or perhaps a knitting project. Then a fluffy gray tail flicked across the old woman's face.

A cat. What a lovely fellow. Ellie ached to stroke the gleaming fur. She hadn't seen a pet like this since they'd left Missouri.

"Hello," she said softly, hoping not to startle the lady or feline. "I'm Ellie Davis, from the farm next door."

The elderly woman gave her a beady-eyed stare from a face as gnarled and weathered as a tree root. Then her head gave a sudden jerk. The eyes snapped shut, head lolling to the side. The cat bounded from her lap and disappeared in the bushes.

Ellie screamed, loud and long, and rushed to the woman's chair. "Oh dear, oh dear. Mrs. Founder, please wake up! Please!" She grabbed the woman's knobby fingers and shook them, gingerly, for they seemed so fragile they could snap at the slightest pressure.

The front door cracked open. "Dearie me, don't mind Grandma." A young woman stepped outside and allowed the door to bang behind her. "She does that when we have new visitors." The girl poked the elderly woman on the shoulder, and Ellie noticed a slight rise and fall of breath beneath the faded lace collar. "We'll leave her here until she decides to behave again."

Holding out her hand, she smiled. "I'm Fern Founder, the youngest of the Founder girls." She seemed a few years older than Ellie.

"Elinore Davis, but you can call me Ellie. From next door." Ellie took the extended hand in a sort of daze. Her experience with elderly folks was rather limited, but she'd never heard of such shenanigans as playing dead when unwanted visitors came around. *Might not be such a ridiculous strategy. Maybe it would work on Mr. Billings.* She almost burst into laughter at the thought of his face.

"Come on inside," Fern beckoned to her. She flipped a dark brown braid behind her shoulder. The plait swished down past her waist, almost to her knees.

"Your hair is lovely," Ellie said.

"Why, thank you," said Fern. "You should see my sister, Iris."

Ellie stepped in after Fern and glanced around the house. She'd expected it to look like most of the larger homes she'd visited, divided by a sort of hallway with a parlor to one side, a sitting room to the other, and bedrooms and kitchen in the back. Instead, a large room opened before her.

A steep wooden staircase–almost a ladder, really–led to a second, loft-like floor. Vegetables and herbs hung in strings and bundles from pegs and nails, giving the house an earthy, wholesome aroma. Colorful quilts of various patterns covered the modest furniture, and a cheerful flame blazed in a large fireplace in the corner of the room.

Three ladies glanced up from various projects around the room. A woman with similar hair and facial features as Fern stood by a massive wooden loom, weaving thread into a design with all the colors of the sunset. Another woman knitted, and yet another with threads of gray in her cinnamon hair, beat a lump of dough on a table's floured surface.

"My sisters, Peony and Myrtle." Fern indicated the weaver and the knitter, who each nodded, smiled, and went back to work. "You may not see Iris. She keeps to herself when visitors come, much like Grandma."

"And this is my mother, Letitia Founder." She led Ellie to the woman with the dough. "Mother, this is Ellie, from next door."

Letitia smiled, laugh lines deepening around her eyes. Her skin was dark, betraying years of work in the sun. "I'm glad you've come to see us. I'd shake your hand, but . . ." She held up dough-covered fingers.

"It's quite alright," said Ellie. "Lovely to meet you, Mrs. Founder."

"How are your brothers?" asked Mrs. Founder. "And your family? Your mother said you'd been working hard to settle in."

"Yes, it's been a tough journey," said Ellie. "I'm thankful to be home."

"Tea?" asked Peony, holding out an earthen cup on a saucer.

"Yes, please." Ellie gripped the edge of the plate. Despite her best efforts to hold it steady, the cup wobbled.

"Where is my sense of propriety?" Mrs. Founder gestured to a nearby cane chair. "Sit, child. Sit and drink your tea."

Ellie obeyed with a deep, contented sigh. The warm peppermint aroma from the tea curled into her senses. Something about the simple, beautiful home with its quiet workers made her want to stay there for always, to join in the peaceful work and allow her soul to rest from the nervous fluttering that seemed to occupy it most days.

She glanced up from her tea. Fern was staring at her with raised eyebrows.

Ellie's cheeks warmed. "I'm sorry. I forgot to mention why I came. My mother sent me over in search of a pumpkin. I have money." She fumbled in her pocket and drew the quarter Mr. Billings had given her.

"Oh, that's more than enough for a pumpkin." Fern waved her hand. "We can throw in a few other things as well. Perhaps some squash and onions?"

"I'm sure those things would make my mother ecstatic." Ellie resolved to try to hide this bounty from Mr. Billings.

"Let me see what we have." Fern started up the steep stairs to the loft. "You can come along, if you like," she said over her shoulder.

Ellie rose, and climbed the steps, balancing her tea carefully.

The loft was filled with bags and barrels of grains, flour, fruits, and vegetables on one side, and four small beds on the other. "My sisters and I sleep there," said Fern, pointing. "Grandma and Mother share a room downstairs, in the back."

Ellie liked the way Fern seemed to anticipate questions before she even asked.

Fern selected an empty flour sack from a stack. "Let's see, we have a nice batch of apples here, good harvest this year. Bet your brothers eat those up before you can put them on the table." She poked them inside. "Here's squash and onions. How about a batch of rosemary? Nice for cooking." The bag became so full, Ellie wondered how she would manage it, along with a pumpkin, for the walk home.

"And you grow all these things here?" she said in wonder.

"Yes. We also have bees."

"Bees?" Ellie's mouth dropped open. "You mean, for honey? How do you keep bees?"

"Mother read some pamphlet written by a man in California who keeps them." Fern wiped her hands on her apron. "Mother's always trying some new idea. She wrote the man and he sent her a bunch of plans. Not only did we have to find the bees, we had to learn their habits and how to keep them alive. If they sting you, for instance, they will die. Did you know that?"

"Doesn't it hurt to be stung?" asked Ellie, in awe.

"Not as much as it hurts the bee." Fern said. "We wear special hats and shawls. They cover us up and protect us from the stings. Anyway, it's worth all the hard work. We supply nearby towns with the best honey in Oregon."

"How did your father like the bees?" asked Ellie.

Fern tied up the top of the bag with a length of twine. "My father died on the trail. We came here when I was only five years old, fifteen years ago, from Iowa. My mother was too heartbroken to marry again, so she and my sisters and I built this farm ourselves. Of course, we eventually hired men to help run the place. In the beginning we were alone."

"That's a wonder," Ellie said. "After knowing what a hard year my father and brothers experienced, it's hard to imagine two women and four young girls attempting the same."

"It was burdensome for us at first." Fern swooped down and put an escaped apple back in its barrel. "We discovered the soil is rich and will give good things if you tend it." She shrugged. "My sisters and I are happy here, and we don't have a man to boss us around. Not that we hate men, mind you. Just haven't found the right ones, any of us. We attend the dances and social functions, rare as they are. Good for business." She sniffed. "Iris won't go, of course. She'd have suitors around the block if she did."

"I see," was all Ellie could think to say.

"What about you?" Fern tipped her head to the side. "Such a pretty girl. I bet lots of men tried to woo you on the trail."

Ellie stared at her hands. She'd tried so hard to push thoughts of Thaddeus away, but he'd show up in her dreams with his gentle smile, playing his violin.

"Oh dear." Fern grasped her fingers. "I'm sorry. I'm far too nosy. It's my worst fault, any of my sisters will tell you."

"No." Ellie waved her hand. "A wonderful man does love me, though I'm worried I might never see him again."

And Ellie found the entire sad story pouring from her lips, things she hadn't told a soul. From the first day she'd met Thaddeus, when he'd helped her untangle her dress from a thorn bush, to that last moment when they'd said goodbye. She left out the tiny, sweet kiss he'd given her. That was hers alone to treasure.

Fern pulled a lacy handkerchief from her apron pocket and handed it to her. "Take this, dear, and dry your tears. Don't worry, I can't see how a man with such a sweet nature could leave you all alone. He'll be back, soon as he's able. I feel it in the tips of my ears."

"Your ears?" Ellie squinted at her.

"Oh yes, that's where I feel things." Fern pulled her hair back to reveal ears that appeared to be perfectly normal, except for the ends, which were a bit on the pointy side. "Mother says the fairies gave me these ears, and I can always sense when certain things are going to happen. Iris has them too. Of course, Iris is . . . really special."

"How . . . interesting."

"We have all sorts of unusual things around here, you'll see." Fern rose and dusted off her apron. "Come back when you can. Your brothers came over all the time. They helped work our crops some, and we gave them food in return."

That cleared up the mystery of how her brothers had managed not to starve. Ellie's shoulders slumped. "My family owes you a gigantic debt," she murmured.

"Not at all," Fern said brightly. "We needed the hands, and they were such cheerful workers. Kind of felt like we had our own brothers for a while." She clasped her hands together. "Oh! I think we shall be tremendous friends, you and I!"

A warmth spread through Ellie's being, like melted wax dripping from a candle. She took the bag from Fern and slung it over her shoulder. "I believe we will."

17
A Tiny Church

Thaddeus's mother dove under the covers, until only her lace-edged nightcap was visible. "You're a hateful boy," she wailed. "How can you leave me when I'm so fearfully ill?"

Thaddeus stepped back to the bedroom door. "You need help I can't give you, Mother. I hope Father will find you a doctor who can do you some good."

Wracking sobs, muffled by the many quilts, was her only response.

"Well, Mother. I love you. I'll write." He left the room and closed the door softly.

Screams followed his wake. He stiffened. *I can't go back. There's nothing I can do.*

He picked up his small travelling bag at the stairs and descended into the front hallway.

His father waited for him at the door, hat in hand.

"I'm glad you've come to your senses, boy," he growled. "Let's get going, the tailor will be expecting us."

"I told you. I'm not going with you."

His father stared at him, cheek muscles twitching. "I've always known you were flighty. Prone to chasing butterflies in your head. I never imagined you'd desert your own father. I've spent my life building a legacy for you. And you're going to chuck it in the waste pile."

"Father, I've told you for years. This isn't the life for me." Thaddeus cleared his throat, trying to will away the thickness. "I hope someday you will understand."

His father's grip tightened around the hat's brim. "If you walk out that door, you will never be welcome to return. Never."

Thaddeus swung around. His sisters stood behind him, tears streaming down their cheeks. He hugged Francie.

"Go with God," she whispered in his ear.

He tried to embrace Maggie, but she ducked away from him, shaking her head.

"I have to go, Magpie. I'll write you. All the time."

Poor Maggie. She's been through so much. God, keep her. Keep her while I'm gone and pour comfort into her soul.

He prepared Ol' Bill's tack with shaking fingers. Grief swept through his soul in waves, but this was followed by peace, assurance. *I'm doing the right thing. I cannot change my family. God has a different path for me, and it's time to follow Him.*

After he'd strapped his pack onto Ol' Bill's saddle, he added his violin, carefully wrapped in a quilt.

Francie ran out to him. "Take care, big brother." Her lips trembled as she handed him a parcel. "Lunch."

"I'll be back to visit." Thaddeus gave what he hoped was a reassuring smile. "As soon as I can. Father will change his mind after he's had time to cool off. In the meantime, I'll write and tell you of my adventures. Maybe someday you can visit my church, when I find one."

"I'd like that. And Thaddeus?"

"Yes, Francie?"

"Say hello to Ellie." She gave him a sly smile. "When you see her, I mean."

Thaddeus grinned. It must have plumb near killed his sister not to mention that she knew of his love.

Ellie. Sunshine hair gleaming in the light, her face tipped back with eyes closed, her hands lifted, as they sang their morning song to God . . .

The sky had remained overcast past noon, and a lone winter bird called from a skeleton tree.

Thaddeus slowed Ol' Bill and came to a stop. He blew on his fingers and rubbed his hands together, trying to coax some feeling back into them.

This Oregon winter was milder than any he'd experienced in Missouri. Back home, his horse would be floundering in several inches of snow. Here, there wasn't a flake to be seen, but still the air was what his father would call 'fairly brisk.'

By his calculations, he should arrive at the small town before the end of the day. He had a map, procured in the town of Roseburg, tucked securely in the brim of his hat. Though his family had come this way a month before, he strained to recognize landmarks and roads. His fingers twitched. *My head was so full of thoughts of Ellie. It's a wonder I made it to our homestead without an injury of some sort. No wonder Father was so annoyed with me. I wasn't much use on that last stretch.*

A farmer's cart clattered beside him. The driver lifted his hat and smiled. Houses dotted the landscape, with acres and acres of fields stretched around them. *Perhaps these folks will come to my church.* It wasn't so crazy, was it? *No. Following the voice of my God has never led me down the wrong path.* He knew he'd come the right way. More than the certainty of his own name.

The town of Oakland didn't have much to boast about. Buildings sagged together like tired old friends. Men meandered here and there, bundled in mufflers and jackets. A saloon stood to one side, colorful faded paintings promising hidden delights. The doors and windows were boarded up.

A pang of doubt entered his mind. If there weren't enough folks to keep a saloon going, would anyone attend his church?

The church building, he remembered, had been within a few streets of the boarding house they'd stopped in for breakfast last month. One more street over . . .

He reined in Bill. The picture had been so vivid in his mind, the actual building jarred him. Though a month had passed since he'd seen it at a fleeting glance, he'd had the tiniest details right, including the boarded windows and the broken front steps.

For the first time since he'd left the new homestead, a bit of doubt twisted his heart. *God, could I make this into anything?*

Isaiah 55:11 floated into his mind. "So shall my word be that goeth forth out of my mouth: it shall not return unto me void, but it shall accomplish that which I please, and it shall prosper in the thing whereto I sent it."

"Your word will not return void," he said to the empty street. He dismounted from Ol' Bill and tied the horse to a nearby post.

The stalwart pillars on the front porch of the church were twined over with dormant grapevine and ivy. Arched windows spoke of loving construction. Peeling paint revealed bare, rotten patches of wood. Thick weeds and brush sprouted on the path and around the building's foundation.

Behind the church, a tiny cottage peeped through thick brush. *Could that be the parsonage?* Thaddeus pushed through the weeds to get a closer look.

Round, brown stones made up the walls, unlike most of the wooden buildings in town. Shingles fashioned from bark covered the roof.

Flat, white stones rose through the tangled weeds, and twisted cedar branches formed a fence around what might have been a vegetable garden once upon a time.

The ramshackle house needed an enormous amount of work. If the roof held true, and the inside wasn't waterlogged, it might be salvageable. Once fixed up, a family could be raised here. Tall trees shaded the home, perfect for trussing up a rope swing like the ones he made a child.

"May I help you?" came a pleasant voice from behind him.

A woman stood on the steppingstone a few feet away. Her snowy hair was tucked up in a smart white bonnet, and she wore a threadbare cloak over a simple taffeta dress.

"Oh, hello." Thaddeus tipped his hat. "Pardon me for trespassing. I came to see the church. I'm Thaddeus Herschel."

The woman tucked her basket over her arm and offered her hand. "Hello there. I'm Patricia Brady."

He pressed the wrinkled fingers carefully. "Nice to meet you."

Mrs. Brady squinted up through thick spectacles. "My husband and I are caretakers for this church and house, although, as you can see, we haven't been able to care for it much lately. Hasn't been a parson for nigh on seven years." She tipped her head. "You seem a mite young to be a preacher."

"I was called at twelve, ma'am," said Thaddeus. "I'm twenty-two now." He stuffed shaking hands into his pockets.

"I see." Mrs. Brady pursed her lips. "And what makes you think this one-horse town is the place you should be?"

"I can't explain it, ma'am," said Thaddeus. "My family and I passed through a month ago. We came from Missouri down the Oregon trail. I saw this place, and I haven't been able to get it out of my mind. I believe God sent me here."

"In that case, you should come and meet my husband," said Mrs. Brady. "You've arrived just in time for supper. Won't you please join us at our table? We've barely a pittance, but it'll fill your belly."

"I'd be much obliged to you," said Thaddeus.

The woman had a sprightly step for her advanced years, almost skipping past the church. She led him down a winding driveway shaded with evergreen trees. A cheery porch with a whitewashed wooden railing awaited.

Two large black dogs rushed to him and sniffed him up and down.

"Don't mind them. You're with me, so you're not a stranger." Mrs. Brady snapped her fingers, and the dogs came to her side, eyes bright.

Thaddeus followed the woman around a winding path to the back door of the home. She wiped her feet on a mat, and he followed suit, wondering if he should remove his heavy, mud-covered boots.

As if reading his mind, she nodded. "You can leave them at the door."

He plopped down on a wooden box and pulled his boots off as she headed inside, the dogs following.

Cracking the door open, he peeked inside. A small kitchen, with a squat iron stove, a table and four chairs. The dogs were already settled in what must be their accustomed places, one on either side of the stove.

The rich aroma of stew filled his senses. He padded into the house in his thick woolen socks, which thankfully had stayed dry.

Mrs. Brady was poking her head through the door. "Matthew, dear, come and meet the new pastor."

"Oh, I'm not sure . . ." Thaddeus began.

Mrs. Brady held up her hand. "You'll have to excuse me. Matthew's hard of hearing. Please sit down at the table. We're not formal here." She darted through the door.

"Matthew, darling, I've brought the bread. Baker had two fresh loaves left, isn't that a wonder?"

Thaddeus stared at the table, set for two, then pulled a chair to a third, empty spot.

"All right, here we are." She bustled back in, followed by a rather portly gentleman.

"Thaddeus Herschel, this is my husband, Matthew Brady."

Thaddeus rose from his seat and held out his hand. "Nice to meet you, Mr. Brady."

Mr. Brady smiled from under a set of impossibly bushy eyebrows and clasped his hand. "Nice to meet you as well, Pastor Herschel. Or is it parson? We've had both."

"Don't forget Reverend Sanders." Mrs. Brady placed a large steaming pot on the table. She filled a bowl with stew and handed it to Thaddeus.

Mr. Brady took a piece of bread and gave Thaddeus the basket. "Yes, I can't forget Reverend Sanders. He only stayed for what, six months?"

Mrs. Brady filled a bowl for Mr. Brady, then one for herself. "Five by my reckon." She sank down heavily in her chair. "Ah. Nice to rest these old feet."

Mr. Brady nodded to Thaddeus. "Would you do us the honor, Pastor?"

Thaddeus smiled. Along the trail, he had slipped into a preaching role easily, since no other man of the cloth had been on the trip. He'd never been formally addressed as such. He closed his eyes and spoke a few simple words of thanks and blessing over the food.

When he raised his head, he was surprised to see tears glittering on Mrs. Brady's cheeks.

She wiped them away with a napkin. "Oh, Pastor Herschel. How we have prayed for you to come!"

Thaddeus lifted his hands. "I'll be honest with you. I haven't been sent by any committee or organization. I simply followed the whim of the Spirit who led me."

Mr. Brady patted his shoulder with a beefy hand. "Though it might seem unusual to you, we've always found our pastor in this manner."

"Or parson. Or reverend." added Mrs. Brady.

"You mean to say, the church has no established denomination?" asked Thaddeus.

Mr. Brady regarded a brimming spoonful of stew with a loving gaze. "Baptist group brought in a minister once. First one we had, actually. Passel of folks came down from Oregon City twenty-five years ago, before the town even had a name. They're the ones built the church and parsonage. When the minister died, they sent another. After that we had, who was he, dear?"

"Methodist fellow," said Mrs. Brady. "Didn't stay long. Moved to a bigger town. Then came others. I don't remember them all. Some with families, some without." She gave Thaddeus a slanted glance. "Do you have a wife, Mr. Herschel? Children?"

"Not yet," said Thaddeus.

"Last fellow was a Methodist Episcopal circuit rider," said Mrs. Brady. "He'd come on the first Sunday of each month. Hasn't been by for over a year. I'd like to hope he moved on to California or somewhere." She chewed a piece of bread and swallowed, her eyes rolling heavenward. "I couldn't know for sure. God bless him."

"All we care about here," said Mr. Brady, "is that the pastor loves the Lord. Do you love the Lord, Pastor Herschel?"

"How can you ask such a question? He presented such a lovely prayer," said Mrs. Brady.

"Still." Mr. Brady gazed at his wife under heavy-lidded eyes.

"Of course," Thaddeus said. "I love the Lord with every part of my being. Without Jesus I would have no breath in my lungs, no purpose to live."

"Can you read, boy?" Mr. Brady asked. "Do you know the Scriptures?"

"First Corinthians thirteen. Though I speak with the tongues of men and angels . . ." Thaddeus quoted the entire chapter.

After Thaddeus finished, Mr. Brady wiped a tear from the corner of his eye. "Beautiful words, made more sacred when a man of God utters them." He beamed. "I suppose there's only one more thing to be discussed. A matter of lodging. And payment."

Mrs. Brady scooped another ladleful of stew into her bowl. "Oooh yes. You'll stay in the parsonage, of course. After we get it fixed up. Until then, you can bunk in our spare room."

"Why, I couldn't possibly..." Thaddeus began, but Mr. Brady cut him short.

"Nonsense, boy, we've already decided."

"Of course we have," said Mrs. Brady, smiling until her eyes almost disappeared under folds of wrinkled skin. "It's providential. I aired out the spare room yesterday."

"For payment, you'll receive what's brought in from the offering," said Mr. Brady. "Might be two bits, might be a dollar. Won't be much. However, folks around here will give a parson odd jobs to help stretch his keep."

"I don't mind hard labor," said Thaddeus.

He munched his last bite of bread. This morning he'd been a scorned son, banished from his family, and now he was a pastor with a church and a flock of at least two.

"Well, what do you say, son?" asked Mr. Brady,

Thaddeus smiled. "Show me where I can keep my horse, and we'll get started."

18
Danger and Direction

"When are you leaving for town?" Ellie asked. She perched on her mother's bed with Heston in her lap. The room Ellie's parents shared was tiny and sparsely furnished, like the rest of the house.

"Soon as I can make myself presentable, which might take a month of Sundays." Mother chuckled at her reflection in the looking glass she'd insisted upon, while adjusting her hat. This was a wide-brimmed straw creation, which sported an enormous bow that completely covered her chin.

The hat was ridiculous, but Ellie didn't say anything. Her mother was proud of the trifle, brought all the way down the Oregon trail and left untouched, in a round, perfect box. Maybe the last nice thing Mother owned.

"You look lovely, Mother." Besides the hat, Ellie's statement was true. Her mother regularly washed and combed her hair again.

She'd sewn a reasonable dress from material she'd procured in town, traded for some of the nicer pelts Robbie had brought home. Her eyes still became vacant at times, and her fingers twitched over invisible tasks. Ellie was sometimes forced to repeat questions several times to a glassy-eyed stare before her mother would respond.

The one time she'd asked her father about this, he'd given a ragged sigh. "It's hard for folks, Ellie. We must love your mother through this time and be patient. Lord knows she's been patient with me." He'd shifted his leg. "We all have wounds that must heal. Try to keep troubles away from her for now, as I do. We must wait until she's strong enough to face them."

What secret troubles he alluded to, Ellie couldn't guess. The problems in front of their faces were difficult enough. The land that must be plowed once the ground thawed in the spring. Clothing for the boys, who'd mostly worn all their garments to rags.

Mother gave the bow a final pat. "It'll have to do." She went into the main room, and Ellie followed, carrying Heston. Ivy, Dave, and Dan were gathered around the fire.

"Your father and I will be back before supper, Ellie." Mother stared into the pairs of shining eyes surrounding her. "Ivy, if you and the boys are good, I'll bring you each a peppermint stick."

The children clapped their hands and skipped around the room. Candy had been an unheard-of luxury for months.

Mother's face glowed with excitement.

But she's leaving me with him. Ellie's stomach twisted. Mr. Billings's eyes glittered at her from the room's corner. As always, he stared at her with that same hunger on his face, like a coyote ready to pounce. His gaze didn't falter as he rose from his seat. "I'm out to chop wood." He ambled to the nails they'd driven into the walls to hold coats and shawls.

"I'm much obliged to you," said Mother. "Tom'll be able to do his share soon."

"I'm sure he will," Mr. Billings said in a cheerful tone. "Until then, I'm happy to help."

After the first troubled glances, Ellie's father had seemed to shrug off any misgivings he had about Mr. Billings. As far as her parents were concerned, the man was a Godsend who'd come to aid them in a desperate time of need while Mr. Davis slowly returned to health.

How can they put such blind faith in a stranger? Especially one that oozed treachery and deceit.

Though she'd had little experience with such men, his agenda had become painfully clear. She'd been careful to avoid him when possible. He'd reach for her hand or touch her hair when they were alone. Nothing quite threatening enough to send her flying to her parents. *If he did something very terrible, would they believe me?*

She'd spent hours outside in the cold, making up chores to avoid him.

Her mother peeked out the window, recently fitted with flour sack curtains. "Children, your father has the wagon ready. Please behave!" She gave an extra wave to Ellie and darted out the door.

Ellie was tempted to run down the steps after her parents and beg them not to leave her alone with Mr. Billings. *Mother is so happy. And perhaps I'm seeing things that aren't true.*

Dan and Dave ran out to find kindling and feed the chickens. Ivy and Heston built miniature cabins out of twigs they'd collected during warmer weather.

Ellie stoked up the fire in the small kitchen stove that had finally arrived and hung a kettle of water to boil over the fireplace. Mother had left a skillet of bread on the table to rise. She punched down the fluffy dough and covered it once more for the second proving.

The door creaked open, then slammed shut. "Kinda nice, ain't it?" Mr. Billing's voice made Ellie jump. "Having some time to ourselves, without your ma and pa around."

"Whatever do you mean, Mr. Billings?" Ellie worked to keep her voice bright and cheerful, pivoting to poke at the stove once more. *Don't let him sense your fear.*

He sauntered over. "It's nice having the house all cozy-like. Almost like you and me are the ma and pa. Wouldn't you like that?"

She slammed the stove door without answering, anger boiling in her hotter than the fire.

He bent closer and curled a tendril of her hair around his finger.

She stiffened, hoping he couldn't feel the slight tremor in her shoulders.

"You'd belong to me, and I'd make sure your ma and pa kept going." He lowered his voice to a whisper. "They'll lose the farm without my help. Best to keep me happy. It won't take much. I'm a simple man with simple needs."

Ellie's gaze darted to Ivy and Heston, who still played, oblivious to the conversation.

Bile rose to her mouth and her head swam. She fought to keep her composure. *I must not anger him.* "Mr. Billings, I'm only eighteen." She forced a short laugh. "My mother doesn't believe I should ever marry. I have a weak heart, you know. I'm destined to be an old spinster."

Mr. Billings placed a hand on her shoulder. "Pretty thing like you has plenty to give a man like me." Dread pooled in her stomach. "I think your mother will be agreeable. And your pa as well."

Ellie jerked away. "I really must peel the potatoes, or they won't be ready for supper."

"Ellie?" Robert stood in the doorway, an axe in his hand. His fingers tightened around the handle.

Mr. Billings strode over to him, towering over the boy by several inches. "Did you finish that woodpile like I told you to?"

"Yes, sir," Robert mumbled. His eyes darted back to Ellie. She gave a slight shake of her head and he exhaled. "Chopped and stacked."

"Good, good." Mr. Billings rubbed his hands together, his knuckles cracking like dead twigs. "We'll want roaring fires this winter, now won't we?"

Robert tilted his head. "I thought you were moving on by Saturday, Mr. Billings. To that business you had in town?"

Mr. Billings grabbed the axe from his hands and studied the blade. "Whatever gave you that idea, son?" He winked at Ellie. "I'll be staying here for quite some time." He went out the door, swinging the axe and whistling.

Ellie sank down on the kitchen stool, her face in her hands.

"Ellie!" Robert rushed to her side. "Are you all right? Did he hurt you, Ellie?"

"No," she said through chattering teeth.

"I don't like him." Robert folded his arms. "Why does Father allow him to be here?"

"You know why." Ellie's cheeks burned. "We need the help, Robert."

Robert threw back his shoulders. "We don't need help from anybody, Ellie. Johnny and I took care of this place by ourselves until you came. We can still handle things."

His eyes, so old in his pinched, boyish face, pierced Ellie's soul. She longed to hold him close and stroke his hair like she would do for Dan or Dave. This would hurt his dignity dreadfully, so she held back.

"Oh, Robert," she finally said. "I think you can manage by yourself . . . soon. I'm worried that Father needs more time to get well. In the spring, the crops must be planted, or we'll lose the land."

"Miss Fern and Miss Iris will help us." Robert lifted his chin. "I've already talked it over with them."

Her brother's lower lip trembled, and Ellie was hit by the unspoken meaning to his words. *They didn't know if we'd make it home. Any of us. They didn't know . . .*

Poor Robbie. He'd prepared to take on the planting, and farming, perhaps even the harvesting, of those massive fields, with only Johnny to help.

"Don't you worry, Robbie," she said, finally allowing herself to reach up and tousle his hair. "You won't be running things on your own. I promise."

Robert moved to the door. "I've got to check the traps. Mr. Billings headed out to repair the fence, or so he said." He lowered his voice. "Look, Ellie. He doesn't really do much. He only works when Father or Mother are watching. He's threatened me and Johnny not to tell, but we really do most of the work."

Ellie pursed her lips. "If that's the truth, then we must figure out how to get rid of him."

Robert pounded his fist into his hand. "Us boys'll give him a whupping."

Ellie giggled at the mental picture. "Let's see if we can figure out another way."

Robert stared at the ground. "I don't know how. He's a dangerous man, Ellie. Even if Mother and Father do realize, I'm worried someone will get hurt." He threw his shoulders back. "I'd better go check those traps. We need all the pelts we can get. Watch yourself."

Ellie eyed the empty space where her father's shotgun usually hung over the front door. Father had taken it in the wagon in case they met up with a winter-hungry bear or wolf on the way to town.

The long-bladed carving knife she hid under her pillow at night hung in its accustomed place by the fire, out of the reach of tiny hands. She took it off its nail and placed it on the table beside her. "Mr. Billings better watch *himself*," she muttered.

She uncovered the bread and settled it deep into the waning coals of the fire.

Thaddeus stepped back and admired his handiwork. Though the whitewash was cheap and stung his eyes, it was a site better than the battered, peeling paint that had covered the church previously. He'd spent two days now, repairing rotten boards, sanding down the roughest areas, and finally covering the building with a fresh white coat.

Mr. Brady had been reluctant to allow him to use the cheap wash, but they simply couldn't afford paint. When the local shopkeeper heard what the coating was for, he'd donated it for free.

After cleaning up the brushes and other tools, Thaddeus entered the church. The inside of the building had been undergoing a transformation as well. Mrs. Brady had recruited every woman in town to dust and scrub the inside, and they'd also weeded and cleared the brush away from the outside.

Ten church pews stood in two rows, worn and scratched, but still sturdy and serviceable. An ornate wooden cross, created by an unknown churchgoer, hung at the back. It gleamed in the light of two windows, one on either side of the room.

Besides these features, there was nothing. No podium to rest his Bible, so he'd built one. No organ for music–he'd have to play his violin. These were small things he could overcome.

He walked to the front, his footsteps echoing in the empty space. As simple and humble as this room was, he could still sense the holiness, the consecration. The years of prayer and sacrifice that had gone into building this house of the Lord.

He swiveled to face the pews. Even in the bareness and silence, the presence of the Holy Spirit was thick and sweet.

"Here I am, Lord." His voice flowed through the room. "You called, and I have answered. If you will send the people, Father, I–I will do my best to shepherd them."

As he closed his eyes, the patient face of his teacher and mentor, Pastor Wilson, floated into his mind. Though the old pastor had been retired for many years, he was always willing to pray with Thaddeus and listen to his many questions. "Remember this, boy," he'd said many times, tapping his wooden walking stick against the floor, much like he'd banged the podium during a particularly rousing service. "It's not how fancy the church is, or how many people walk through the doors. It's how you care for those the good Lord entrusts to your keep."

Thaddeus sank to the wooden planks that had been smoothed and worn by the feet of hundreds of believers before him. "Thank you for what you've done. This is the dream you've planted in my heart. Please help me not to fail you, Father." He paused. "And please Lord, let me be worthy of Ellie."

He pressed his fingers against his temples. *Would Ellie ever want such a life?* Her father had given her a comfortable home, before they journeyed from Oregon.

Two months had passed since he'd kissed her goodbye on the trail. He'd written her two letters, one from the homestead, and one from the Oakland parsonage, but he'd heard nothing back.

What if she found someone else?

A tear dripped down his nose and splashed on the floor.

A peace flooded through him, the peace that was beyond all understanding and imagination.

"Lord, I know you are with me, and somehow, I will carry out your work. You've brought me to this time and place for a reason, and I will trust in you."

He opened his eyes. Mrs. Brady stood in the door; her bent frame bathed in the golden light of late afternoon.

"Sorry to disturb you," she said softly. "Supper's ready. My husband says a cold wind is blowing in, and he wouldn't be surprised if we had snow tonight, so good thing you got the roof fixed and painting done."

"Thank you." Thaddeus rose.

"Pastor Herschel, you've worked so hard." Mrs. Brady's lips trembled slightly. "I just don't want your feelings to be hurt if we only get a trickle of folks at first. Of course, we'll have the women in town, the shopkeeper, and the postman. The people from the outer farms, well, it'll take time for the news to soak in. And once the snow comes, people tend to burrow in like bears in hibernation. They'll all be out again, come the spring. We might have a bit of a slow winter."

Thaddeus patted the elderly woman on the shoulder. "Don't worry, Mrs. Brady. I'm willing to wait for the flock. I'll be content ministering to those who come."

19
Fireside

The dark and cold of falling dusk had driven everyone to huddle beside the fire in the Davis home, including, to Ellie's chagrin, Mr. Billings. Though he had the small stove in the barn, the building was far from weather-worthy, and her mother and father had invited him to partake of the warmth in the house. Of course he had agreed, after only the slightest, probably fabricated, hesitation. He roosted in the corner on one of the new chairs he'd built, reading his everlasting newspaper.

Ellie glowered over her embroidery, which now sported three small drops of blood where she'd pricked her finger in absent-minded irritation.

That morning, she'd tried to broach the subject with her father. He'd been outside, checking their gelding's hooves. He'd listened to her list of concerns with patient eyes. "He's a man, Ellie. You're a pretty girl. I'll speak to him. He probably doesn't realize he's making you uncomfortable. Some men don't."

She'd wanted to scream and throw every pot and pan in the kitchen. Get on the ground and beg her father to chase him away. *What would we do? How would we manage?*

Her trusty carving knife hung from its usual hook. She'd sneak it into her apron pocket on her way to bed, as she always did. It was getting easier to picture herself pulling it out, driving it into the human being that threatened her. She hated that she'd become that kind of person. What other choice did she have? The only people who saw what she endured were Robert and Johnny, and they slept in the loft above.

A cheery rap sounded on the door, jostling her from these dark thoughts.

"Who on earth could that be?" Mother set her mending down in her lap.

Robert stood and glanced at Mr. Davis.

"Go ahead, son." Mr. Davis put the shovel handle he'd been sanding to the side and folded his hands in his lap.

Robert opened the door. Fern and Myrtle stood on the doorstep, lanterns glowing in their hands.

"We've come by," they both said at once, then giggled.

"We've come by," Fern continued, "to borrow Ellie for a few hours. We are having a party by the fire and we'd like her to attend."

"Oh, couldn't we come along?" Johnny begged.

Mr. Billings didn't say a word, but he leaned forward with clasped hands.

"Only us ladies tonight," said Myrtle. "We promise to have a Christmas party for all the good little girls and boys of the house soon. Christmas is only two weeks away, you know."

"My goodness, is it that soon?" Mother asked in an innocent tone, her cheeks pink.

Ellie gave an inward chuckle. She'd been helping her mother make Christmas mittens and wooden tops and decorations for weeks now.

"Yes, ma'am." Fern's elfin mouth pinched up at the corners. "Mightn't we borrow Ellie for tonight?"

Mother nodded to Ellie. "Do you feel strong enough to walk to their house in this cold?"

"Mother, I'll be fine," Ellie said firmly. She wished her mother would remember that she hadn't had a fainting spell in over six months. *Is it impossible for her to see how strong I've become?*

"You may go," said her father. "Be home in two hours."

Ellie pulled on a coat and wound a scarf around her head. Shoving her feet into boots, she fairly danced out the door, despite her heavy garb.

Fern and Myrtle locked arms with her on the path, and they skipped down the moonlit driveway, as though they were schoolgirls and not grown women.

"Oh, this is delightful," said Fern. "Myrtle said you'd never be allowed to come, and I said, well, at least we should try."

"I'm glad you did," said Ellie. "I needed a break from that stuffy room. And Mr. Billings." She shuddered.

Myrtle wrinkled her nose. "I can see why you dislike him. I met him at the post office. He makes my skin crawl."

"Why exactly is he staying at your house?" asked Fern. "Is he your uncle, or your second cousin once removed, or something like that?"

"No, not related," said Ellie. "He helps with chores. Sometimes."

Myrtle wrinkled her nose. "If that's the case, why did he tell the postmaster he was family? He was checking for mail when I saw him."

"That's strange," said Ellie. "I don't remember him giving her any mail. Who would write to us?" *Unless . . . Thaddeus?* The thought made her cold all over, beneath the stuffy coat. *Ooooh.* She clenched her fists. *If Thaddeus wrote me and Mr. Billings stole my letters . . .*

"I know it's un-Christian of me, but he's a slimy, odious man and I wish he would leave."

Fern and Myrtle stopped and stared at her.

"Why would that be un-Christian?" asked Fern. "Iris has a gift for discerning people's character, and she believes that man is an absolute snake."

"Why would it be un-Christian to want a snake out of your home?" asked Myrtle. "I've found snakes in our house. The good ones get a good shaking and the venomous ones get their heads chopped off." She paused. "Not that I'm suggesting you do *that*."

"I-I suppose when you put it that way, it makes perfect sense," said Ellie.

The Founders' home, like the Davis cabin, had a blazing fire in the grate. But the house was cozy and filled with good-natured hope. The difference was tangible the moment Ellie walked through the door.

Mrs. Founder motioned to an ornate hat-rack standing by the door. "Hang up your things and come sit a spell. We'll make popcorn and roast nuts. We have a pile of apples over there if you'd fancy one." She pointed to a basket on the table.

Peony, sitting at the fireplace, waved with one hand while industriously shaking the popcorn popper with the other.

A woman, thin and wispy as a willow-wand, rose from her place by the fire and held out a slender hand to Ellie. "I didn't meet you last time." Her gray eyes sparkled with a thousand lights, and her smoke-like hair was tied in a careless knot at the nape of her neck. "I'm Iris."

"El-Ellie."

Iris's gaze deepened. "Tethers. Binding you every which way. One could come and free you, but he is hindered."

"I . . . how did you know that?" Pins and needles pricked at Ellie's skin.

Fern laughed. "Goodness sakes, Iris, you've scared the poor girl to Easter. Don't worry, Ellie. Like I said, Iris has a gift for knowing things about people. She's had it since she was a young girl. We are Bible-believing women of faith here, and in the Bible there's all sorts of prophets and seekers who are able to hear the voice of God."

Iris nodded. "I'm sorry if I gave you a start, Ellie. Sometimes the words are so strong that I forget to hold them back."

Ellie let out a deep breath. "That's all right. It's a wonderful gift."

"I'll be praying for you," said Iris. "For freedom."

"Thank you," said Ellie, staring down at the shining red russet apple someone had thrust into her hands during the conversation.

Granny rocked in the corner with the same fluffy cat in her lap. Tonight, though, she seemed in good spirits. She raised a gnarled hand in greeting, with no signs of faking her death again.

They sang old songs, including a few of the hymns Ellie had been taught by Thaddeus. The popcorn and nuts disappeared rapidly, and all the women took turns telling old stories and jokes. Mrs. Founder read tales from the worn copy of One Thousand and One Nights she took from the mantle.

Pictures of princesses and flying carpets and magical lamps flashed through Ellie's mind. She settled into the chair's bearskin covering, basking in warmth and comfort and friendship.

Someone touched her arm. Fern peered down with a smile.

"Sorry, Ellie," Fern whispered. "You fell asleep and no one noticed the time. Mr. Billings has come to fetch you."

All the beautiful moments were quenched from the night, as though a pail of freezing water had been tossed over them.

Ellie sat up straight. "I can't walk back with him," she whispered.

"Don't worry," Fern whispered back. "We'll be right behind you, Myrtle and I."

Ellie rose on shaky feet. Mr. Billings stood at the door; his eyes fixed on her.

She darted a look at Fern, who in turn gave a meaningful glance at a rifle that hung over the mantle.

Fern gave Mr. Billings a flirtatious smile. "How gentlemanly of you to walk Ellie home. We've had a lovely time tonight, haven't we, Ellie?"

Mr. Billing's mouth was set in a hard, firm line. "You shouldn't have stayed so late, Ellie. Your mother was worried."

Mrs. Founder drew herself up. She made a rather imposing figure, with her work-thickened shoulders and standing almost as tall as Mr. Billings. She looked him square in the eye.

"Mrs. Davis should know Ellie is safe with us. We may be a house full of women, but we know how to handle ourselves, sir." She gave Mr. Billings a glare that made the hairs on the back of Ellie's neck stand on end.

Ellie realized then the gumption that had carried these women through the last fifteen years of survival. Strength and endurance had been forged through the hardship of the trail, like many others, and instead of allowing it to break them, they'd found the ability to run a farm and built a life better than many men could do.

The trek home, though perhaps unpleasant, would be safe.

She put on her coat and scarf and hugged each woman goodbye, except for Iris, who gave her a little wave instead, and the grandma, who clutched her cat and gave her a toothless grin.

Mr. Billings held out his elbow. Ellie pretended she didn't see it and stepped past him, down the porch steps and across the trio of steppingstones that led to the driveway.

Suddenly the moonlight, which had seemed so magical and cheery, took on a darkened edge. The evening birds were silent, and a chill wind rushed around her head, poking cold fingers under her scarf.

"Why won't you take my arm?" Mr. Billings said, once they were away from the house. "The way is full of rocks and holes; I would hate for you to twist your pretty ankle."

"Leave me alone." Ellie was tired of Mr. Billings. She was tired of living in a state of anxiety, pretending all was fine. She wanted, more than anything, to have rest and sleep in her life again, instead of jolting awake with sudden creaks of the house.

"You didn't have to come fetch me," she snapped. "Robert knows the way."

Before she could move, Mr. Billings grabbed her wrist and pulled her around to face him. "You know why I came for you," he said. Moonlight poured over him. The hungry leer she'd come to expect from him passed over his face. "Your mother was anxious. I didn't know if those women had invited farmhands to their party. I'd be worried for you. You're too young to understand what goes on in the minds of common men."

"Common? Like you?" the words flew from her mouth before she could stop them.

Angry flames rose to his cheeks and his grip tightened. "I'll thank you not to speak ill of me again," he hissed. "You will come to respect me. In time. I'm willing to wait." He let go of her arm.

She stumbled down the path ahead, refusing to give him the satisfaction of letting him see her rub the skin where he'd gripped so tight.

Tears stung her eyes, but she lifted her chin. She wanted so badly to scream, to tell him she would never, ever belong to him. A cold helpless fear crept over her. Though he didn't push for a kiss or something more tonight, he could try again any time. He'd been welcomed into their home. Her parents valued his physical strength more than they cared for her happiness and safety.

A twig snapped behind her, and she smiled wanly. *Mr. Billings should count his blessings.* If he'd hurt her, two angels with rifles would have dropped him in his tracks.

When they reached the house, Mr. Billings wordlessly left her at the porch steps and sulked off in the direction of the barn.

She tripped on the welcome mat and almost fell through the front door.

Mother sat by the fire alone, the endless pile of torn trousers beside her. She glanced up and pushed the work aside. "Ellie, what on earth?"

"Oh, Mother." Once the words were out, Ellie couldn't hold back the racking sobs that burst from within her. She ran to her mother's chair and laid her head in her lap like she'd done when she was little.

Mother stroked her hair. "Child, what's got you in such a rumple?"

Ellie swallowed and wiped her face with her apron. "Mother. Please ask Mr. Billings to leave. I don't ask you for much, Mother. Please."

Mother cupped Ellie's chin in her hands, but her eyes were glazed over, as usual. "Ellie, what's gotten into you all of a sudden? Mr. Billings has helped us so much in this difficult time."

Any hope Ellie had been holding onto drained away into the desolate floor beneath her feet. "No, Mother. He is not good." She held out her arm where he'd grabbed her on the driveway. A red mark had formed, which would surely become a bruise. "He did this to my arm. He wants to marry me. I hate him."

Mother laughed; a dry chuckle Ellie recognized as one she reserved for a child who had tried her patience, but she still saw as amusing. "Oh, Ellie. What an imagination you have. I'm sure Mr. Billings didn't mean to hurt you. He doesn't know his own strength, is all. He does like to flirt and joke around, but as I've said before, he was like that with all the women on the wagon trail. Besides, the man's thirty years old if he's a day. What would he want with a weak child like you?"

Ellie took a deep, shuddering breath and rose from the floor, her hands clenched at her sides. "Very well. If you will not believe me, I'll have to watch out for myself."

The carving knife gleamed in the firelight, and she took it down from its place.

She glanced at her mother. Mother's eyes were closed, and she hummed to herself, holding the mending close to her bosom as though it were an infant.

20
A Chilly Lunch

A fresh blanket of snow covered the fields, pure and untouched except where small creatures had scavenged for food. Ellie skirted the edges, trying to avoid making an obvious path of her own. She checked over her shoulder to make sure Mr. Billings wasn't somewhere in the white terrain, watching her. The snow crunching under her feet seemed loud as a thunderstorm.

Ten days until Christmas. As promised, the Founder family had hosted a delightful Christmas party for the Davis children, with all the fruits and nuts and sweetmeats the children could hope for.

The Christmas presents in their own home, including a new rag doll for Ivy, had been finished and hidden under blankets in her mother's trunk to await the big day. But Elli

e wasn't excited for Christmas this year.

She climbed the crude board fence of the cow pasture, then headed to the left portion of the property, which remained as wild and untouched as it had been for centuries.

In this corner she'd discovered a pond, surrounded by willows and cottonwoods. Boulders of all shapes and sizes framed the edges. Even with the cold and death of winter, the pond was a beautiful place. A sturdy branch would serve to break a hole in the thick ice, and if she stayed moitionless, sometimes she'd see deer and other animals come to quench their thirst in the frosty waters.

Fern waited on a flat rock in a patch of sun that had melted away the snow. Her blue and red skirt bloomed against the eggshell-hued stone, and her usual braid was wound into a chignon and tucked into a snood.

She waved. "Hello! Glad you could come today."

"Hello." Ellie perched on the rock beside her friend. "I couldn't find much for lunch. Mother baked gingersnaps yesterday. I also brought a chunk of fresh bread."

"Lovely." Fern pulled out a small jar of pickles. "I have these and smoked ham."

"Pickles!" Ellie exclaimed. "I haven't had pickles in a month of Sundays, as Robert says."

"I'm glad I brought them, then. This is an especially good batch." Fern held up the jar and studied the green globs inside. "We'll give you cucumber seeds in the spring. Then you can make some next year."

"Mother will be happy. She loves pickles even more than I do. She won prizes at the fair for them."

"I wish we had fairs here," Fern said wistfully. "I've never been to one, but my older sisters have told me about them."

"No fairs? That'll disappoint Mother, though she'll have enough to keep her busy come the spring."

The two friends ate in content silence while the winter birds chirped to each other in the trees across the pond.

Ellie appreciated this about Fern. While her friends from school days, and even Maggie and Francie, filled the moments with endless chatter, Fern seemed to enjoy the silence as well.

After swallowing the last bite of pickle, Fern spoke. "How are you holding up with . . ." she lowered her voice. "The evil man?"

Ellie brushed crumbs off her lap into the hole she'd broken in the ice's surface and watched them float on the surface of the pond until they disappeared into the mouths of unseen fishes. "I ignore him as much as possible. He's waiting me out. I'm positive he plans to stay for spring harvest. He'll make a big show of working so hard that Father will have to agree when he asks for my hand."

The corners of Fern's mouth turned down and she jabbed at the rock with a stick. "Do you really believe your father would say yes?"

Ellie swallowed hard. "If you'd asked me that question a year ago, I would have said no. But now . . . Father acts like a different man. Even though he's regained much of his strength, he's still so broken inside. He goes along with whatever my mother says. If she says yes, he might agree."

Fern stared at her, concern creeping into her deep brown eyes. "What about your preacher fella? You gave him your address, didn't you? Why can't he thunder in to rescue you?"

Misery pooled in Ellie's soul. "I don't know. I was worried Mr. Billings might be stealing his letters, but I finally received a note a few days ago, he'd sent in October. They'd just arrived home at that time. It takes mail so long to get here."

"Did he say when he would come?" asked Fern.

"No. He said he missed me." Heat crept into Ellie's cheeks, despite the cold day. "His words are beautiful, and I know he must care for me a great deal to say things like that. His family needed settling. He wants to make sure he has a plan. A home for us. I don't know what he's going to do."

Fern twisted her hands in her lap. "Can't blame him for trying to figure things out. Most preachers I know are fairly poor, Ellie."

"I don't mind being poor," Ellie said. "All I want is to be by his side, helping folks. It's all I've wanted my whole life. To care for those who need it most and share God's love with the lost."

She rubbed her forehead. "If he did come, how could I leave my family in this state?"

Fern placed a hand on Ellie's arm. "You may not have a choice, if Mr. Billings truly plans to take you for his own."

This was true. Ellie would rather die than be with the horrible Mr. Billings her entire life. But to run away from her family, her brothers and sisters, forever, without so much as a blessing, was an equally unimaginable fate.

Fern continued. "Your parents chose to have seven children. They chose to come to Oregon and build a home here. Your path may go a different way. You have every right to find happiness on your own."

Fern packed the empty pickle jar and other remnants of the picnic and stood. "My sisters and I keep you and your family in our prayers. You'll find a way out of this, I'm certain of that."

"I hope you're right," Ellie mumbled. "I'd better get home. They'll have noticed I'm gone by now."

"And by them, you mean Mr. Billings," said Fern.

"Yes." Ellie gave her friend a quick hug. "Thank you for listening. And praying."

Thaddeus faced the pews once more. A handful of people stared back at him. The sparse congregation was comprised of two couples, including Mr. and Mrs. Brady, a few single farmers, and one family with two adorable but impish-looking boys.

He'd just finished playing Silent Night on his violin, and the musical notes lingered in the air, filling the church with their somber, sweet tones. Peaceful smiles covered the work-worn faces, and tears slid down more than a few cheeks.

As Thaddeus opened his worn, heavily marked Bible that had made it all the way through the Oregon trail, he gazed out over the congregation. "We will be reading Matthew 2:9 today."

Mr. B55204rady was the only person who appeared to have a Bible, and Thaddeus waited as the elderly man fumbled to his place.

Thaddeus cleared his throat. "This is the story of wise men, who came from a country far, far from where Jesus was born. These men were diviners, the Bible says. We don't really know what that means, but they did search for signs in the sky. And one day, they noticed a star. A bright, beautiful heavenly body that moved through the sky, leading the way to a country they had never visited. Through the Holy Spirit, they knew this foretold of a child being born. A child that would save the world."

He read the beautiful old words, not bothering to try to keep the wonder from his voice. 'When they had heard the king, they departed; and, lo, the star, which they saw in the east, went before them, till it came and stood over where the young child was.'"

"Can you imagine?" Thaddeus asked the congregation. "A glowing thing in the sky, something no one had ever seen. These men felt this shining orb would lead them to a savior. To the King of Kings and the Lord of Lords. And they followed it."

He held out his hands. "My question to you. Will you follow the Master? Would you follow Him when and where He calls? When you hear the still, small voice in your spirit, or when He calls your name in the night?"

Several members of the congregation began to nod their heads.

"Perhaps He won't send a star to tell you of His will. It might be a Scripture verse. It might be in the song of the sparrow. The Bible says, 'His ways are higher than our ways.' We won't always understand. If we stay close, we will know the voice of our Father. And when He speaks, we must obey."

The rest of the sermon came tumbling from his lips. In a heartbeat, it was time for the closing prayer.

As he stood at the door, the father of the two young boys came up and gave him a firm handshake. "I'm Zeke Miller. Good sermon, Pastor. I'm not quite sure what you were getting at, but it sounded mighty fine just the same. Mighty fine."

Thaddeus was accustomed to folks who didn't understand his messages. Some people had a hard time grasping the concept of God the Father, who lived among and within His people and worked as provider and healer, far past Biblical times. A father who loved and forgave and dealt out second chances.

"I'm glad you enjoyed the sermon," he replied. He pulled a scrap of paper and a bit of pencil from his pocket. "I'll write down the verses from today. If you have the will, take some time to meditate on the scripture. Seek the Lord for revelation."

A grin spread across Zeke's face beneath his bushy beard. "I got a Bible at home. I can read some and my wife reads better. We'll do that, Pastor."

Mrs. Brady took his hand, her face shining beneath the dusty berries and flowers of her Sunday hat. "Would you come to lunch, Pastor?"

He bowed his head. "Normally I'd love to. Today I feel the need for solitude. Perhaps next week."

After the church was empty and silent again, he ducked out the back door and out to the parsonage.

With the stir of preparing the church for Christmas, the humble cottage hadn't been fixed up as much as he'd like, but it was clean, weather-proof, and livable. Thaddeus appreciated the stone walls and the cozy, round fireplace. It had two bedrooms, a combined kitchen and living area, and a small larder with a tiny window up by the ceiling.

After the constant chatter and activity during the months on the trail, Thaddeus appreciated a quiet place to ponder and pray. Though being alone also made him face the rash decision he'd made to leave family and comfort for this tiny church.

His simple meal of bread and cheese was soon finished, and he settled in the old rocker by the fire. December winds howled at the wooden shutters and he made a mental note to tie them down when the weather got better to spare himself the noise.

Though the churchgoers had been few today due to the cold, the town had been kind and welcoming. His tiny larder was full of canned vegetables and fruits and dry goods. Generous housewives and farmers had seen to that. He'd been able to find work weather-proofing homes and barns, as well as help caring for stock. All in all, he needed nothing.

Nothing but Ellie.

The thought pierced his mind like an icicle, fallen from a roof and driven into snow. He ached for her. Playing his violin had become a strange mix of comfort and pain, for each time he drew his bow across the strings, he was reminded of her.

She would love the tiny church; of this he was sure. *Can I ask her to join me in this life? I have no future to offer. We may never have more than this small group of people attend the church. God has called me here, but how can I presume she'd be called to the same place?*

His head slumped to the side, and he fell into a fitful sleep.

Dark shadows played behind his eyes. Ellie was dancing, twirling like she did on the campfire nights when he'd play his violin to lift people's spirits. Her eyes were closed, her hands lifted, that beautiful smile he knew so well settled on her face, like a hopeful butterfly.

The fire. She stood too close. He tried to call out a warning, but the words wouldn't come as flames licked the hem of her dress and swept up her waist. Her joyful expression changed to one of pain and terror.

He awoke with a jolt. A cold gray pallor had crept over the waning sunshine, and the threat of snow hung in the air.

A crumpled note rested on the fireplace mantle, one that he read every day, though he'd memorized it long before. He stumbled to his feet, still sleepy, and grabbed the paper.

"My father's address is Hilltop Lane in Cottage Grove. Please come for me. I'll be waiting."

His mouth turned up on one side. She was so trusting. So completely giving of herself. There were no conditions to be met, nothing to be proven. In his heart, he knew she still waited for him. *She's in danger.* Of this he was more certain, even than the snow that would fall in hours, perhaps moments. The time had come, and if he didn't go now, something terrible would happen. *Perhaps it's already happened.*

He grabbed a satchel and stuffed it with what meager supplies he owned. No time to go to the store for provisions. Good thing the church members had been so generous with food. Two towns lay between Oakland and Cottage Grove, and at least a day and a half of riding if the weather didn't slow him down.

He'd have to find shelter in a barn or shed for the night. He certainly couldn't afford a boarding house.

"I'll sleep in the snow if I have to," he muttered angrily. *Why, oh why did I wait so long?* He knew as sure as he breathed Ellie was meant for him, and him for her. Why couldn't he trust that God would care for them?

He saddled Ol' Bill, who snorted his disapproval.

"I know, it's crazy to go out in this weather," he said, puffs of fog appearing as he spoke. "I have a promise to keep, and I've already waited too long."

He knocked on the Brady's front door and gave a hurried explanation.

Mr. Brady's impossibly large eyebrows bristled. "Yer leaving us a week before Christmas? Surely you'll be back in time."

Thaddeus bowed his head. "You've both been so good to me and given me all the faith I could ask for. Someone I love needs my help, and she's more precious to me than all the world. If I don't go now, she could be lost. Please understand, I'll return as quickly as possible."

Mrs. Brady came up behind her husband, two steaming potatoes in her hands. "Put these in your pockets. They'll warm you for now and feed you later."

"Thank you." Thaddeus tipped his hat. "I'll be back by Christmas, if I'm well and fit to do so."

He mounted Ol' Bill, clouds pregnant with snow, looming over him. As they headed to the main road, he prayed, "God, please protect me and keep back the worst of the weather. Keep Ellie safe, and help me get there in time."

21

Let No Man

Three days until Christmas. Ellie cut a star from a piece of polished tin and tied on a string to hang it from the window. A few flakes of snow fluttered past the glass like tired moths.

Through the clouded glass the barn loomed, taunting her. She must do the evening milking. Robbie and Johnny hadn't returned from the trapline, Ivy hadn't quite mastered the technique, and Mother was in bed with a headache.

A plan had formed in her mind, wrapping around itself like a ball of yarn, growing larger and larger until it threatened to hop out of her mind and right out on the floor.

Eugene. A few days ride from here. Where Jerusha had planned to go. *She'd take me in, I know she would*. The day after Christmas, Ellie planned to pack her bags and slip away. Yes, the road was dangerous for a single woman on her own. *Could it possibly hold a greater terror than life with Mr. Billings?*

The cow only gave a few cups of milk now. The butter was nice to have, and if they didn't keep milking, she'd dry up in a short time.

Normally she'd make sure Mr. Billings was away, but tonight lantern light shone through the outline of the barn door. *He won't be going anywhere this late.*

Her belly sagged, as though she'd eaten lead for supper. She stepped down from her stool. Grabbing her thickest wrap, she pulled it tightly around her. "I'm going for the milking."

Her father glanced up from his book. "Haven't you already gone?"

"No, I wanted to finish decorating the window since the little boys were asleep."

"Don't slip on the snow." Her father gave her a level gaze. *How can he be so blind?*

Bracing herself for the blast of cold air, Ellie opened the door and rushed outside.

Swirling snowflakes glowed in the lantern light like frozen fireflies. Ellie grabbed the pail from the porch and headed into the barn. She cracked the door open. *Maybe he's already asleep.*

"So you've come to see me, eh?" Mr. Billings lounged on a chair he'd fashioned from scraps of wood. He'd spent time painting the inner room beneath the loft, and even built a bookshelf from a crate.

She wondered how she hadn't noticed these changes. They'd come slowly, bit by bit. This was a place for someone battening down the hatches, staying for a long haul.

Reality hit her like a deadly dart to her soul. *He's never going to leave. He'll bide his time, like he said, until he's ready to demand what he wants, and Mother and Father will hand it to him, because they'll have no choice. They are beholden to him like they've been to no other.*

Her skin went cold, and despite the chill in the barn, she began to sweat. She lifted her chin. *I will not let him see my fear.* She didn't say a word, just bent to wipe down the cow's udder with her warm cloth from the house.

"I'm talking to you, girl," Mr. Billings growled. He gestured to the blanket beside him. The milking can wait. Why don't you warm up by my fire?"

"No, thank you," she said, sending streams of milk into her bucket.

He rose, a terrible leer on his face, and before she could move, he'd stomped through the hay until he stood beside the cow. His breath hit her full force, even from several feet away.

He's been drinking. Where did he get the whiskey? Probably his last trip to town. Even their small village had one of these dens of iniquity, and she had no doubt Mr. Billings was the sort of man that would frequent such a place.

"Remember what I told you, girl," he slurred. "I'll teach you to respect me. And you might as well, because you are going to be my wife. I'm telling your pa on Christmas Day." She rose on shaking feet. The rough boards of the stall wall dug into her back through her thin shawl and dress. His glowering bulk blocked the only exit. *Why, oh why didn't I wait for Robert to come home so he could milk for me? I wouldn't have wanted him here either, not with Mr. Billings drunk. Oh God, please save me from this man.*

"Seeing as how you're going to be mine, how about a kiss?" Mr. Billings said, inching closer. He grabbed her wrist so tight she winced.

The cow shifted, knocking him a bit off balance.

Ellie used the movement to wrench free. She lurched toward the stall's opening.

Despite Mr. Billing's inebriation, he beat her to the exit. "Ah ah ah," he said, waggling his finger at her. "Naughty girl. You aren't getting by without my Christmas kiss." A growl crept into his voice. "Remember, girl, you owe me. The weeks of work I've put into this place, all for your folks. Why, those children would have starved if it weren't for me."

"We would have managed," said Ellie from between clenched teeth.

"Why, you ungrateful wench! You're gonna show me some gratitude!" He grabbed her shoulders and pushed her against the wall. Gone was any sign of the air of dashing and debonair persona he put on for strangers. He was all wolf now, filled with the need for power and control.

And I'm the prey. She flattened herself against the wall, and like a wild creature, held perfectly still. *Please, God. Please send someone. Someone who can help.*

"Ellie?"

The barn door cracked open, and a man stepped through. His face was covered by a muffler, dusted in snow. Only his eyes peered out.

Her heart stopped for several beats. She knew those eyes and that soft-spoken voice. It couldn't be. *How* . . . She must be dreaming. She'd wake up, any moment, back in Missouri.

Mr. Billings spun around, once again letting go of her shoulders. "What the–Who's that?"

Thaddeus pulled off the muffler. "What are you doing here, Billings? I don't think Ellie appreciates your attention."

"She's going to be my wife," snapped Mr. Billings.

Thaddeus's eyes widened, and his skin flushed from pink to a sickened pallor.

Ellie tried to protest, but her jaw tightened, and she couldn't speak. Time was frozen, and she would be forced to stare into those tortured eyes for the remainder of her life.

Mr. Billings drew himself up and stepped toward Thaddeus. "You're that preacher man from the wagon train. What the blazes are you doing here?"

"On a mission from God," said Thaddeus. "Or so I thought." His gaze lingered on Ellie's face. "Are you in love with this man?"

Ellie found her voice. "No, Thaddeus, no!" She began to sob, and stumbled past Mr. Billings, into the arms of the man she loved. "You came!" she cried into the frosty material of his jacket's shoulder. "You finally came."

The cloth was cold and damp, but she didn't care. A hand stroked her hair, and he wrapped his other arm tightly around her. "I wanted to get things ready for you," he said, his breath warm on her ear. "I didn't know . . ."

Different hands, rough and hard, pulled at her shoulders, wrenching her away. "Get away from him!" Mr. Billings screamed. "You belong to me!"

Her body slammed into the barn wall, and she slid to the floor, stunned. A flash of light and pain rushed through her head, and she fought to stay conscious, to pull herself up. *Thaddeus might get hurt,* she told herself, as though she were patiently explaining to a child.

Through her foggy eyes Mr. Billings rushed Thaddeus. Thaddeus raised his fists in defense. The two men crashed together, fell to the ground, and struggled in the hay.

Mr. Billings grappled at Thaddeus's throat. "You should have never come back!"

Thaddeus twisted and kicked the older man off his chest. He flipped over and held him down. "You're drunk, Billings. Why would Ellie want to be with a man who hurt her?"

Ellie cried out, but her words came in weak whimpers. When she tried to move, bright colors flashed before her eyes.

Mr. Billings pulled his hand free from Thaddeus's grip and threw a punch. His fist crunched into Thaddeus's nose. Dark blood splattered in the golden hay.

A pitchfork leaned against the barn wall. Ellie crawled over to it and *there!* Her fingers closed around the handle. She scrambled to her feet and swung the tool at Mr. Billings's head.

The infernal man ducked and grabbed the pitchfork's tines. "What are you . . ." He glowered at her like an angry coyote interrupted at a meal.

He scrabbled for something at his waist and yanked out a gleaming knife. Holding it high, eyes wild, he inched closer.

Thaddeus crouched on the floor, blood pouring from his nose. "Ellie . . ." he croaked.

Once again, Ellie found herself against the barn wall, breathing hard. She winced as the knife flashed into the air and closed her eyes, waiting for the dreadful bite . . .

"Put the knife down, Billings."

Ellie opened her eyes. Her father stood in the barn door, framed by the inky darkness, his rifle in his hands.

Mr. Billings returned the knife to its sheath and stepped back. His wolfish smile spread across his face, and he held up his palms. "I would never hurt your daughter, Mr. Davis. You know that." He pointed to Thaddeus, who had moved to Ellie's side. "This stranger attacked her. I came to her rescue."

Something wet dripped down Ellie's forehead. She touched it and then stared at red, sticky fingers. Suddenly the numbness was gone and in its place, a deep rage reared its head, boiling hotter and stronger as it grew.

"Thaddeus is not a stranger," she said, every word sending a sharp pain into her head. "He was on the wagon train with us. He's a dear friend, and–and I love him, Father." She pointed to Mr. Billings. "Though I've tried to explain, you wouldn't listen. He wants me to marry him."

Ellie's father's jaw dropped. "Do you want to marry him?"

"I'd rather run barefoot through a field of angry prairie dogs," said Ellie. "Father, he did this to me." She pointed to her head. "And he's hurt Thaddeus."

"He did, did he?" Her father raised his gun higher. "Mr. Billings, if that is your true name, which I am beginning to doubt. I would never force my daughter to marry a man she didn't love. As for paying you back for the work you've done ... be grateful I don't fill your good-for-nothing hide with bullets."

Mr. Billings opened his mouth, then closed it again. He glanced at Ellie, then Thaddeus, and then slowly stepped back towards his area, darting a look at his possessions.

"No, I will gather your things," Ellie's father growled. He handed his rifle to Ellie. "Don't take your eye off that man."

"You're hurt, Ellie," said Thaddeus from across the barn.

"I'll be fine," replied Ellie, though pain still smarted behind her skull.

Mr. Davis grabbed a burlap feed sack and stuffed it with books, clothes, and a blanket. He thrust it at Mr. Billings. "That's what you get, and be happy to have it."

Mr. Billings took the sack with a curse. "I need to fetch one more thing. You owe me that much."

"I owe you nothing," Mr. Davis growled.

"It's right up here, in the rafters." Quick as a squirrel, Mr. Billings darted up the ladder to the hayloft.

A shot cracked out through the barn loft, and the rifle jumped in Ellie's arms.

Mr. Billings flew back down the ladder and landed on the ground, a satchel in his hands.

All three men stared at Ellie, who looked down at the rifle.

"I . . . you moved," she said to Mr. Billings.

Her father touched a fresh bullet hole in the side of the barn. "And a good thing you were quick on your feet, you ingrate. Otherwise she'd have blown a hole the size of a dinner plate in your heart." He sidled up next to Ellie and took the rifle back. "It's time, Mr. Billings. Get off my land and don't you ever come back."

"You'd send me out into the cold, dark night?" Mr. Billings whined. "Without a horse or lantern?"

Mr. Davis rubbed his beard. "Hmmm. Perhaps you're right."

He nodded to Thaddeus, who'd finally managed to quench the blood flowing from his nose. "See that coil of rope hanging yonder?"

Thaddeus grabbed the rope.

"Tie that fellow's hands," said Mr. Davis.

Thaddeus tied Mr. Billings's hands together in front of him, pulling the knife from its sheath and pitching it into the hay while he did so.

"Now," said Ellie's father. "We'll be taking a wagon ride to town. Ellie, you go inside and get your mother to help bandage your head. And mister," he nodded to Thaddeus. "You may come along. Perhaps on the ride back you can tell me why you'd be worthy of my daughter's love."

22
Put Asunder

Ellie leaned on Thaddeus, her head still swimming. She ignored the pain, focusing on the realness of his presence, his scent. The rise and fall of his breath. Things she couldn't feel in dreams.

"I've missed you so dearly," she murmured.

"I'll leave you for now," he whispered at the door. "I promise to be back as soon as we're sure Mr. Billings is on his way. Your father doesn't mind leaving him in the cold, but the man will be a lot less likely to come back and cause trouble tonight if we escort him into town. We'll try to turn him in at the sheriff." He squinted up at the sky. "We'll hurry. Looks like a storm's rolling in."

Ellie wanted to clutch at him and beg him not to leave, but her father couldn't handle Mr. Billings by himself, not in his condition. He'd be doing well just to make it to town.

"Go," she said, staring into his eyes. "You'd better come right back to me, Thaddeus Herschel."

"I will. I promise." He brushed her cheek with the faintest of kisses. Then he headed down the porch steps and across the yard to the barn.

Ellie stepped into the house and closed the door.

Mother leapt from her chair. "Ellie, you're bleeding! What happened? Where is your father? I woke up and the house was empty except for the littles."

Ellie sank down at the table. She leaned back in the chair and closed her eyes. "He went to town, Mother."

"Went to town!" Mother dampened a flour sack in the washbasin and began dabbing at Ellie's forehead. "A storm's coming in! What in the world would he be going to town for? And Mr. Billings. . ."

Ellie caught her mother's wrist in a gentle but firm grip. "Mother, Mr. Billings is the one who did this to me."

Her mother stepped back, her eyes bulging. "What do you mean?

The tears Ellie had shed a few weeks ago on the walk home from the Founder's house were gone now. The anger that had surged through her when Mr. Billings had thrown her against the wall had also left her soul, replaced by a calmness she'd never felt. She said a quick, silent prayer before she spoke.

"Mother, I love you, and always will. And I forgive you for making decisions from a place of desperation. You came here and found Father weak, and you needed help getting ready for winter." As she spoke, waves of peace continued to flow through her. "I tried to tell you Mr. Billings was dangerous. I showed you when he hurt my arm. You didn't believe me, and you refused to protect me. Thaddeus has come."

"Thaddeus . . . Herschel?" Her mother dropped the flour sack.

"Yes. And I love him, Mother. He loves me." Ellie stood, supporting her weight on the table until the room stopped spinning. "He's taking me away, and I will marry him."

"Ellie," Mother's fingers crept to her lips. "You have no idea how difficult it is to be a wife. How will you bear children? With your heart so weak."

Ellie lifted her chin. "I am not weak. I trudged over hill and dale, for almost six months, from Missouri to our homestead here. I carried your children in my arms. I cooked meals and hauled water. I'm fully capable of being whoever God has called me to be."

Mother wiped her eyes, and her chin quivered. "You're right, Ellie. I shouldn't have doubted your word. You are a woman now. I should have realized that."

Picking up the flour sack once more, she dabbed at the blood on Ellie's forehead and stepped back to survey her work. Tears glistened on the tired, sallow cheeks that had been so round and rosy before they left Missouri. "There. It's a small gash, and the bleeding has stopped. You'll be all right. Thaddeus is a good man, Ellie." Her voice caught, and she looked away. "I hope he'll take care of you. I believe he will."

"God will take care of both of us," said Ellie.

The door swung open and Robbie and Johnny came in, covered with snow.

"What happened to you?" asked Robbie.

"Mr. Billings knocked me against the barn wall." Ellie marveled at her own matter-of-fact tone.

Robbie whipped a bowie knife from his belt. "You let me at that yellow-bellied coward! I'll kill him, sure."

"Put the knife away, my son," said Mother. "Your father and Thaddeus are taking him to town."

"Who's Thaddeus?" Johnny wrinkled his nose.

"He's the man I'm going to marry." Ellie's spirit leapt anew at these words.

Robert's mouth dropped open. "Marry? Since when?"

"Since when he asks her," said Mother. "You boys miss a lot when you come home late. Go on to bed now. We'll sort out all these issues in the morning."

###

Mother suggested Thaddeus stay in the barn where Mr. Billings had slept. Ellie agreed that would be for the best.

The two women worked by the fire–Mother with her mending and Ellie with her embroidery.

A stick shifted in the coals. Mother and Ellie shared an anxious glance.

Mother snapped a thread with her teeth. "Oh, I do wish they'd come back! You'd think they'd have returned already, wouldn't you, Ellie?"

Ellie opened the door and shone a lantern into the yard. "Snow's falling, but only a little, like it's been all night. I'm going to prepare Thaddeus a place in the barn and stoke up the fire, Mother."

"All right, might as well do something."

Ellie found a fresh blanket, the only one they had to spare, and headed outside. She paused at the barn door, took a deep breath, and crept in.

Deep ruts from the previous struggle crisscrossed through the hay, and a smear of blood trailed along the barn wall where she'd hit her head.

The feelings that had been so elusive during the conversation with her mother now flooded through her in an overwhelming force, and she fought the urge to curl up by the stove and cry herself to sleep.

Thaddeus will be tired when he gets back. He just rode through the cold for who knows how long to find me, and now he's got another freezing ride back from town.

She gathered her broiling thoughts together and went to set Mr. Billings's former living area to rights. Whatever vices the man possessed, he'd at least kept a tidy space.

She fluffed the pallet from the floor, spread it back out, and covered it with the fresh blanket.

Firewood was stacked in a corner of the barn, and she threw in a few logs. The flames flickered merrily in the stove's belly, and she spread her freezing fingers out to warm them.

Now that the initial fright and pain had passed, elation trickled into her heart in breathtaking jolts. *Thaddeus will be back, and he's never going to leave me again! Wait until I tell Fern.*

Fern would be missed greatly, but of course they would return to visit. She'd come to see her family anyway. *Leaving Robert, and Ivy . . .* She lifted her chin. It was time for a new adventure in her life, and she would return before they missed her.

Her shoulders sagged. *How can I go?* Her father was still not well. It was unfair to leave her brothers and mother with the winter chores, *and then the planting . . .*

Reluctantly, she moved away from the fire. Time to go back inside. Thaddeus would find a cozy place to spend the night, at least, even if she'd have to destroy him by refusing his hand. Her head pounded. *I'll die if I have to tell him no. God, why have you put me in this horrible position?*

As she stumbled to the barn door, something glinted in the firelight, over by the ladder to the hayloft.

Reaching down, she pulled it from the sand. A ten-dollar gold eagle. It must have fallen from Mr. Billing's pocket. *How did he possess this kind of money?* She pursed her lips. Hopefully it wasn't his last coin. No one from her home would be riding back to town to return it. And she doubted he'd be sending any letters to let them know where to send it.

She slipped it into her apron pocket. *Maybe he'll be in jail. Not much to spend money in there.*

Wagon wheels crunched through the snow outside, and she rushed out the barn door. Sure enough, only her father and Thaddeus were in the wagon. Overwhelming relief flooded over her. *I'll never have to see that terrible man again.*

Thaddeus jumped down from the wagon and pulled her into his arms. "I missed you," he said.

Ellie caught her father's eye over Thaddeus's shoulder, and her father nodded and smiled. "He's a good man, Ellie."

"Mr. Davis, I'll get the horse settled. Why don't you go in and get warmed up," said Thaddeus.

"I'll help you," said Ellie. "Both of you must be frozen to the bone."

"Anger has a way of heating you up." Mr. Davis dismounted from the wagon stiffly. "I'll go on in and let you young folks do the work. Need to speak with my wife anyhow."

Thaddeus and Ellie quickly unbuckled the harness and led the horse to her stall in the barn.

"I fixed up the room in here for you," said Ellie. "Sorry you have to sleep out here. However. it's fairly cozy and not as stuffy as the house."

Thaddeus glanced around, a smile spreading over his face. "This is nicer than the shed I slept in last night, I promise you that."

Ellie finally had a chance to ask the most pressing question out of the many that buzzed through her mind. "What made you come here? In the snow of all things?"

Thaddeus ran his finger along her cheek. "I know you'll understand. That's why I love you, Ellie. God told me to come. I was going to wait until spring at least. I have a church ..."

"How wonderful!" Ellie clasped her hands.

Thaddeus held up a finger. "The building is tiny, and the congregation is small. I've been working odd jobs to keep food on the table, though folks deliver meals as well." He bowed his head. "It's not much of a place for a wife, yet."

"Oh Thaddeus, I'll be happy anywhere, as long as I'm with you," Ellie said. "The only problem . . ." Her lip trembled. "I can't leave my family until Father is better."

Thaddeus stared down at her. "I don't know how I could leave you now. You've had such a long hard struggle. I hate to drag you into something even worse."

Ellie stepped back, heat rising to her cheeks. "Nothing could be worse than what I've been through the last few months. I'd go back to the Oregon trail if it meant missing out on that."

"I'm so sorry you had to endure what you did." Thaddeus's cheek muscle tightened. "Your father feels terrible. He blames himself. The man has been extremely ill. He chewed ol' Mr. Billings up and down on the way to town." He rubbed his chin. "I might have given him a few choice words of my own."

Ellie thrust her hand into her apron pocket, and her fingers closed around the gold coin. She showed it to Thaddeus "I found this in the dirt. Figured it belonged to Mr. Billings, but I don't know how we can return it to him."

Thaddeus laughed, flipped the coin in the air and caught it. "Oh, yes, we didn't tell you. We took Mr. Billings to the sheriff's office. He wasn't too happy about that, tried to light a shuck and escape from the wagon. We chased him down, the sheriff and me. You know that bag he climbed up to retrieve? He had a bank's worth of gold holed up in there. Seems he's wanted from here to Nebraska, robbed a trading post back in June. He's been swindling folks in wagon trains ever since."

"He's locked up?" Ellie exclaimed.

"Yep. I watched the sheriff turn the key." Thaddeus tucked the coin into his pocket. "I'll give this to your father to take into town. I'm sure the trading post folks will be happy to get it back. In fact, the sheriff said your father might be seeing a substantial reward, got up by the various posts he's robbed."

"That would be wonderful," said Ellie. "We'd better go inside and see what my parents are discussing."

Ellie's father met them at the door. "I've been explaining things to your mother."

Mother gave them a bright smile, though her eyes shone with tears. "Thaddeus, I'd be happy to have you for a son-in-law."

"Mother, how will you cope through this winter?" Ellie asked.

"Don't you worry." Ellie's father put his hand on her shoulder. "Your mother is amazing with money, child. You may have done without some things on the trail, but now she has a nice little nest egg left over. We'll use some of that to hire a hand or two until I feel better."

Mother nodded. "I spoke with Mrs. Founder yesterday, and she told me if we ever needed help, she could recommend some decent, hard-working fellows. Not only that, but there's the reward." He put a hand on Thaddeus's shoulder. "I'll be sharing that with you, son."

Ellie pressed her hand against her chest. "This has been the strangest day. I might burst from this joy."

Thaddeus caught her up in his arms. "Say you'll marry me, Ellie?"

"With all my heart!"

23

Happiness

"What therefore God has brought together, let not man put asunder."

Reverend Caulder closed the Bible and beamed at Thaddeus. "Now you are forever joined as one."

Thaddeus took Ellie's hand, marveling at the warmth of her skin, the sweet thrill her touch brought to his soul. *I am my beloved's and she is mine.* Only in this moment could he truly understand the joy of that bridegroom in the ancient book. *She is mine.*

Reflected on her face was the same joy. They turned and faced a roomful of smiling faces.

Each item of furniture in the Founder family sitting room was occupied, and a few of Ellie's siblings sat on the floor or laps. Fern and Iris had draped holly and pine wreaths over the mantel and window frames, and bouquets of dried flowers filled vases in every corner of the room.

Though Thaddeus had only just met the Founder family, he could see why Ellie had become friends with them so quickly. They were kind, generous souls who had offered their home the minute they heard of the wedding.

The only faces missing were those of his family. Though it saddened him deeply, he and Ellie had decided it would be better not to wait for his father's permission, which would probably never come. They'd write the Herschels to tell them the news, and perhaps visit in the spring and hope for a reconciliation of some kind.

"Now, we must celebrate." Mrs. Davis came and took his hand. "It's a pity you didn't bring your violin."

"Isn't it though?" said Thaddeus. "I didn't know I'd need it. Though I'm afraid it wouldn't have fared well in the weather."

"Never mind," said Fern. "Grandma plays the mouth harp."

Sure enough, the old woman pulled out an instrument from somewhere in the mounds of knitting in her lap and set it to wizened lips.

A sweet tune issued forth, and soon furniture was moved, rugs were rolled back, and folks began to dance, even little Heston, who rode around on Ivy's feet.

Thaddeus whirled Ellie to the tune. Who would have ever thought a week ago, as he gave his Christmas week sermon, that he would be here? With a beautiful woman on his arm. The only woman he'd ever want to be there. His wife.

After two dances, Granny Founder announced she was all out of breath. The guests adjourned to the dining area, where a feast from the Founders' vast winter stores had been spread.

Mrs. Founder stood at the head of the table with a goblet of cider. "To Ellie and Thaddeus," she said, her face glowing in the light of dozens of beeswax candles. "You have found love. The most beautiful, painful, wonderful thing you could ever hope to find. Don't ever let it go."

Ellie reached over the ornate napkin on the table, which had been embroidered within an inch of its life, and squeezed Thaddeus's hand. "Never," she whispered.

"Never," he whispered back, wondering if his soul might burst from the joy.

Much later, after many thanks had been given and Ellie had given tearful goodbyes to Fern and her sisters, Thaddeus and Ellie walked back down the path to the Davis cabin.

Nothing could have made the day better. Except for my family. I wish we could have reached them in time. Thaddeus sighed. *Maybe someday they will accept the choices I've made. A life of wealth and leisure was never what I wanted.*

Ellie snuggled into his shoulder, her breath warming the skin of his neck.

"Are you happy?" he asked her.

"Happier than words could ever express," she replied.

"I'm glad the snow has stopped." Thaddeus said. "We'll be back to the church before Sunday."

"I can't wait to see the parsonage," said Ellie. "I'm already planning what I'll plant in the garden for spring."

"Don't expect much," Thaddeus warned. "It's warm, at least."

Ellie tilted her head back, blue eyes dancing. "You'll be there, my love. And that's all I really need."

Ellie pulled the blankets, provided by the kindly coachman, tighter around her. Though they carried a faint aroma of sweat and dust, she was thankful for the warmth.

The wheels came to a shuddering halt, and Thaddeus lifted his head. "Are we there already?"

"Maybe. You've been sleeping for hours. I didn't realize I was marrying such a lazy man," Ellie teased.

Thaddeus gave her a sleepy smile. "You're here. With me. It's real."

"Of course I'm real."

The coach door swung open and the driver peered in, his head and coat covered with powdered snow. "We're here, folks, and a good thing you came when you did. Real squall of a blizzard coming in."

"Thank you, sir." Thaddeus climbed out, took Ellie's small case from the coachman's hand, and tipped his hat. "I'll return for my horse in a moment."

Ol' Bill shook his mane and nickered from where he'd been tied to the back of the wagon.

"Take your time," said the driver. "I'm going t'the inn for supper." He untied the horse and led him to a hitching post under an awning. "He'll be here when you want him."

"Much obliged," said Thaddeus.

Ellie wrapped her fingers around the crook of his arm, and he led her through the ankle-deep snow down the path to the church.

She stopped short as they passed the building. A blanket of snow covered the roof and steeple. Even though the cut-glass windows were dark for now, the place still glowed, like it held wise and beautiful things just waiting to be discovered. "It's breathtaking, Thaddeus."

He rubbed his jaw. "You should have seen it when I arrived here. The townsfolk helped fix it up."

Ellie clapped her hands, despite the thick muff she wore. "I want to see inside!"

Thaddeus tipped his head to the side. "Would you rather see the house first?"

"Yes, please!" Ellie replied. *Our house.*

"And we'll have to tell the Bradys, of course," said Thaddeus. "Won't they be surprised?"

"The Bradys? Who are they?" asked Ellie.

Thaddeus slapped his forehead. "Don't tell me I haven't mentioned the Bradys! Oh well. It's not like we've had time in the last few days, planning a whirlwind wedding and all. They're the caretakers here, live a ways over there." He gestured to the road.

They approached the small house. "Wait here," said Thaddeus. He opened the door and set the trunk and his bundle of belongings inside. "All right." He came back out. "Close your eyes."

Ellie obediently covered her eyes with her hand.

"I'm starting this off properly," said Thaddeus. "Be it ever so humble."

And with that, she felt his arms sweeping her up.

"Thaddeus, what on earth?" She laughed and wrapped her arms around his neck.

Being carried was a strange sensation, like she was weightless.

In a moment, she felt the warmth of a fire to one side, and the aroma of fresh bread filled the room.

"That Mrs. Brady, God bless her," said Thaddeus. "Her faith in me was so strong, she built us a fire and brought dinner."

"All right." He placed her down on the hard-packed floor with a kiss. "You may open your eyes."

The room was tiny, for sure, and a thin pattern of cracks ran up the wall above the fireplace. But the fire burned cheerily in a lovely earthen stove, and the window was in the perfect place above the washbasin so she could look out while she was cooking.

She turned to him, hands clasped and eyes shining. "Oh, Thaddeus. It's our very own. Our very own little home. Just for us."

"You're happy then?"

"More than words can say." She flung herself into his arms.

"I'm with you. And together we'll make this the loveliest home Oregon has ever seen."

The End

About the Author

Angela has been writing stories since she created her first book with a green crayon at the age of eight. She's lived all over Central Texas, mostly hovering in and around the small town of Bastrop Texas, which she loves with unnatural fierceness and features in many of her books. Angela has four wild children, a husband who studies astrophysics for fun, and a cat.
To find out more about her writing and learn how to receive a FREE short story, go to
http://angelacastillowrites.weebly.com